MICHAEL PEARCE was raised in Anglo-Egyptian Sudan, where his fascination for language began. He later trained as a Russian interpreter but moved away from languages to pursue an academic career, first as a lecturer in English and the History of Ideas, and then as an administrator. Michael Pearce now lives in South-West London and is best known as the author of the award-winning *Mamur Zapt* books.

Praise for Michael Pearce and the *A Dead Man in …* series

'His sympathetic portrayal of an unfamiliar culture, impeccable historical detail and entertaining dialogue make enjoyable reading.'

Sunday Telegraph

'The steady pace, atmospheric design, and detailed description re-create a complicated city. A recommended historical series.'

Library Journal

'Effortlessly funny and engaging. Packed, as ever, with fact, flavor and the kind of insouciance which makes history lighter than air.'

Literary Review

'Picking up a new book by Michael Pearce reminds you why people enjoy reading mysteries.'

Denver Post

The A Dead Man in … series

A Dead Man in Trieste
A Dead Man in Istanbul
A Dead Man in Athens
A Dead Man in Tangier
A Dead Man in Barcelona
A Dead Man in Naples

A Dead Man in Athens

Michael Pearce

SOHO
CONSTABLE

Soho Press, Inc.
853 Broadway
New York, NY 10003
www.sohopress.com

First published in the UK by Constable,
an imprint of Constable & Robinson , 2006

First US edition published by Carroll & Graf, 2006
This paperback edition published by Soho Constable,
an imprint of Soho Press, 2009

ISBN 978-1-56947-610-9

Printed and bound in the EU
1 3 5 7 9 10 8 6 4 2

Chapter One

That was another of the things he used to think about as he stood there in the grey light of dawn waiting for the barrage to begin. How had it got to be like this? And if he had known, could he, Seymour – since he didn't believe in blaming other people when the world went wrong – an ordinary police officer in the East End of London, have done anything to stop it? Or even part of it? The aeroplanes, for example? He could hear it now, as he stood there, the irritating, gnatlike buzz of the spotter-plane coming to take up position and call all hell down from the skies. Could he have stopped that? Stopped Stevens, say. But, of course, someone *had* stopped Stevens and it hadn't made any difference. The barrages had still gone on. But had there been a moment when it might all have been averted? That moment, for example, in Athens in the autumn of 1912.

It all began, unpromisingly, with a cat.

'A cat?' said Seymour disbelievingly.

'That's right.'

'Surely I've not been sent out from London to invest-igate –'

'Well –'

'It was a very nice cat,' said the Second Secretary, molli-fyingly: 'one of those blue-eyed ones. Angora, I think you call them.'

'Yes, well, maybe, but –'

'The Sultan was very fond of it.'

Sultan? Wait a minute, where was he? Surely they didn't have Sultans in Greece?

'What Sultan is this?' he said cautiously.

'The one in Istanbul. Only he's not in Istanbul now. He was sent into exile. First to Salonica, then here.'

'With the cat,' said the Second Secretary.

'And his wives. Some of them, that is.'

'And the cat's been poisoned?'

'That's right.'

'Well, I'm very sorry to hear it. But, look, is it really necessary to send a police officer all the way from London –'

'Oh, yes. It's rather important, in fact.'

'To investigate the death of a cat?'

'Most definitely. You see, it's not just the death of a cat.'

'No?'

'No. It's widely thought that the cat was a sort of sighting shot for the Sultan. Cat first, Sultan next. And the Sultan's been complaining of stomach pains.'

'Well, I can see that's more serious. But – Look, what the hell's it got to do with Scotland Yard? Or the British Embassy in Athens, for that matter?'

'We're suspected of having had a hand in it.'

'Of poisoning the cat?'

'And maybe the Sultan. Nonsense, of course. But that's what people here are saying. So, it's important to sort this out as quickly as possible.'

'Find out who *did* do the poisoning,' said the Second Secretary.

'Yes. Yes. I can see that. But – I'm sorry, but I still cannot see why it was necessary to send to London for a detective. There must be police out here –'

'Not trusted. Look, old boy, if it wasn't us who did it – and I can assure you it wasn't – then who was it? The Greeks, think the Ottomans. So they're certainly not having a Greek to do the investigating. And vice versa. The Greeks think the Ottomans did it. So the last person they want doing the investigation is a Turk. And the same with the others.'

'The others?'

'The Bulgars.'

'The Macedonians.'

'Montenegrins —'

'Serbs —'

'Slovaks —'

'Et cetera. Welcome to the Balkans, old boy.'

'No one trusts anyone,' said the Second Secretary.

'But why should they trust the British any more —'

'Oh, they don't. But we happened to have a warship out here and were able to knock heads together. In the end they saw the merit of an independent investigation.'

'But I rather gathered from you that they didn't think we *were* independent? That we'd actually done the poisoning ourselves?'

'Oh, they didn't like it. But what with the warship being so handy —'

'It took some time,' said the Second Secretary, 'but eventually it was agreed to send for Scotland Yard. And they sent —'

'Me,' said Seymour. Not altogether happily.

'The obvious choice,' said the Commissioner, and sighed.

Seymour was the obvious choice because he was about the only person in the police, or England, for that matter, who had any command of foreign languages. It made him an odd bird at Scotland Yard; which accounted for the sigh.

For Seymour definitely was an oddity. He wasn't, for a start, in his colleagues' view, properly English. He maintained he was, of course, and pointed out that his grandfather had come to the country fifty years before, and that both his father and he himself had been born and bred in the country. But his grandfather had originally been named Pelczyinski and his mother, Karolyi, which was one of the things that had given him access to other languages.

The other was the fact that he had grown up in London's immigrant East End.

'I see you have Greek,' said the lordly soul at the Foreign Office who had interviewed him before allowing him to depart for Athens. 'Where did you acquire that? Winchester? Oxford?'

'Whitechapel,' said Seymour unflinchingly. 'There are a lot of Greeks in the East End.'

'Good Lord!' said the man from the Foreign Office, aghast. He had hesitated for a moment and then: 'That would be demotic Greek, I suppose, not classical?'

'Greek as it is spoken today, yes,' said Seymour.

'Well, I suppose that could be useful,' said the man from the Foreign Office doubtfully and he had quickly moved on to other subjects.

That was not quite how old Tsakatellis, the shopkeeper from whom Seymour had learned most of his Greek, had spoken.

'The Greek language, my boy,' he had said, frequently, 'is one of the glories of the world. It was the first great language of civilization; and its time may be coming again.'

Similar claims, however, were made by the Italians, Jews, Germans and Poles living further along the street and Seymour was inclined to apply a general discount to such claims. The fact was, though, that whatever might be the case at the ancient universities, in the East End foreign languages were alive and kicking, and it was there, as a boy, going round with the police interpreter, that Seymour had first acquired them. They were, of course, useful to any policeman working in the polyglot East End. But they were also useful when the rare call came for a policeman who could work abroad.

'But why,' asked Seymour, 'would England want to poison the Sultan? Never mind the cat.'

'To start a war. Or stop it, depending upon your point of view.'

'War?' said Seymour incredulously.

The First Secretary got up and beckoned him over to the window.

'Do you see those flags?'

'Yes.'

'Anything strike you about them?'

'Only that there are a lot of them.'

'You probably saw some on your way from the port?'

'Yes. The streets were full of them.'

'Anything else?'

'Well, there are a lot of soldiers about. And bands. But I thought . . .'

'What did you think?'

'That it was a festival or something. A Greek national festival.'

'It will probably turn into one,' said the First Secretary grimly, 'if they win the war.'

War? How was it that Seymour hadn't heard about this? It hadn't been in any of the newspapers. Surely he couldn't have missed it on his way to the sports page?

'But – who are they going to be fighting *against*?'

'The Ottomans. Turkey. And that, of course, is where the Sultan comes in. And the cat.'

'The *casus*,' said the Second Secretary.

'What?'

'*Casus. Casus belli.*'

Latin, in fact, was not among Seymour's languages. But he got the drift. The cause of war.

* * *

9

Around the corner, as he made his way to the hotel after leaving the Embassy, came a herd of goats. It was the second herd that he had seen. This one stopped in front of a house and a woman came out carrying some pans. The herdsman selected a goat and milked it straight into the pans, filling one after another. Then the herd moved on.

'The Athens milkman,' said the Second Secretary, who had obligingly offered to show him to his hotel. 'Not like ours, of course. There are cows, up in the hills, but the Athens woman prefers goat's milk. More reliable in hot weather, I'm told.'

'The cats, presumably, prefer goat's milk, too?' said Seymour.

The Second Secretary looked startled.

'I have never considered the point,' he said.

Off in the distance he could hear a bell clanging. The clanging came nearer and round the corner charged a new electric tram. Seymour was impressed. He hadn't expected to find anything like this down in Athens.

The goats scattered, plunging into nearby doorways. The herdsman shook his fist at the tram and shouted abuse. The driver, on his platform, grinned and then clanged the bell triumphantly.

'The old and the new,' said the Second Secretary. 'Of course, all places are. But Athens is older than most.'

Up on the hill Seymour could see the Parthenon, its columns clear against the blue sky. Old Tsakatellis had spoken about this, too.

'A sacred spot for all Greeks,' he had said. He had looked sternly at the young Seymour. 'It ought to be sacred to you, too,' he had said. 'This is where democracy began.'

Seymour had nodded his head. Democracy, he knew, was a good thing. Later he found that not a lot of it spread to the Whitechapel police station. Still, now, he looked again at the Parthenon, and with respect. This was where it had all begun. And so long ago, too! A sneaking doubt crept in. Ought it not to have got a bit further by now?

The tram clanged away. The herd reassembled – and then scattered again as another vehicle came speeding round the corner. This time it was a motor car. Seymour had not seen so many motor cars in his young life, even in London, as not to have his eyes drawn. It shot in and out of the traffic, between the horse-drawn carriages, with their drivers shouting imprecations, around the heavy ox-drawn carts with the ubiquitous mysterious hand painted on their sides, perhaps to ward off the evil eye, or possibly, these days, the ever more evil motor car, and braked sharply – and fortunately – at a line of bewildered donkeys, each piled high with grapes. Then off it shot again, leaving a great cloud of dust and people spluttering in its wake.

Dust. That, in the end, was Seymour's abiding impression of Athens. When the motor car had passed, he had expected the dust to settle down. It didn't. It just hung in the air. Whenever it looked inclined to settle, something always came along to disturb it. There was a thick layer of dust on the road – in fact, the road *was* dust, and it was perpetually being stirred by the feet of the donkeys, the oxen, the horses and the passers-by, not to mention the goats. When it did settle, it settled in a thick film that covered everything, including the new lightweight suit of Panama cloth that Seymour had just splashed out on.

His shoes were thick with it. That, no doubt, explained the omnipresence of bootblacks. All along the road and gathered in thousands at every café and hotel and outside all the big shops were small boys, who banged their brushes together noisily to attract custom and who would dash out into the street to whisk the dust from your boots even as you walked along.

'It's the wind,' said the Second Secretary. 'And the drought. The wind blows the topsoil off and then everything below dries to dust. And there are no trees, of course. They've not had time to grow.'

'Not had time to grow?' said Seymour, looking up at the Parthenon, which seemed pretty old to him.

'Since Athens was chosen as the new Greek capital about seventy years ago. When Greece gained her independence from the Ottomans. Most of what you see about you has been built since then. It's like walking through a new town.'

'It's like walking through a desert,' said Seymour.

At the entrance to the hotel small boys rushed forward to flick the dust from his shoes with long feather brushes.

The Second Secretary halted.

'You'll want to give yourself a bit of a sponge-down, I expect,' he said.

Yes, indeed. And to wash the dust out of his hair and from behind his ears and out of the corners of his eyes, not to mention shaking it out of his pockets and out of the turn-ups of his trousers and from the folds of his handkerchief.

'And have something to eat, I'm sure,' said the Second Secretary. 'But be up bright and early in the morning because you've got to meet Dr Metaxas.'

'Dr Metaxas?'

'And go with him to the mortuary, where he'll run through with you the details of the post-mortem.'

'Post-mortem? On whom?'

'The cat, of course.'

When Seymour came down the next morning a tall, thin figure in a dark suit was pacing nervously up and down in the foyer.

'Dr Metaxas?'

'Mr Seymour?'

They shook hands.

'Have you had breakfast? No? Well, don't. Do what every Athenian does.'

He took Seymour to a café in the central square where

hundreds of people sat out at tables starting the day as they meant to go on: slowly.

Almost all the tables were already occupied but Dr Metaxas found his way to one which wasn't and where he was apparently known, since people at the adjoining tables greeted him. He sank down into a chair with relief and at once a waiter brought coffees. He put them down and looked at Dr Metaxas.

'Yes?' he said enquiringly.

'Yes,' said Dr Metaxas.

'And for the gentleman?'

'Ouzo?' asked Dr Metaxas.

'This early?'

The doctor shrugged.

'No, thanks,' said Seymour.

The waiter brought Metaxas a small glass of ouzo and the table a plate of sweet cakes. Seymour didn't fancy the cakes, either, but this, it seemed, was breakfast.

He had just picked one up when people at all the tables around him began to stand up. Cab men rose on their boxes, small bootblacks stiffened to attention. Even inside the café people were getting to their feet. Everyone was rising.

Except Dr Metaxas.

A band marched past followed by some soldiers carrying a flag. People took off their hats. Dr Metaxas stayed put.

The band went off across the square and came to a halt outside a large building on the other side.

'The Palace,' said Dr Metaxas. 'They're changing the guard. We have this rigmarole every morning.'

They all sat down again.

'I don't believe in palaces,' said Mr Metaxas. 'Or kings, either. As you see, I am in a minority.'

The doctor's sympathies were apparently well known since no one seemed to take umbrage. Seymour caught, indeed, a few grins at surrounding tables.

'In any other country,' said Metaxas, 'including,

13

I believe, your own, the monarch is treated with indifference. Only in Greece is he taken seriously. While this was understandable initially – when we became independent it was pardonable to demonstrate enthusiasm for having a ruler of our own – to persist with it is folly. It is a betrayal of the deep democratic instinct that makes the Greek special.'

He looked challengingly at Seymour, as if expecting his dissent.

'Yes, my Greek friends in London say something similar,' said Seymour.

'Ah, you have Greek friends in London?'

'Indeed.'

'Let us drink to such friendship!'

Seymour felt he could not demur this time, and the waiter brought two glasses.

And then two more. And then two more.

'What about the post-mortem?' said Seymour, after a while.

Metaxas brushed it aside.

'Post-mortem? On a cat? Ridiculous!'

He waved a hand to the waiter again.

Seymour began to feel unhappy.

'You don't think –'

Metaxas glared at him.

'I,' he said, 'am a medical practitioner from the School of Medicine at Athens. My business is healing people. Not animals. If they want an animal looked at, why don't they ask a vet? Why do they ask me, Metaxas? It is an insult. Not just to me, but to Greece! The Sultan, yes, his body I would examine. With pleasure. Very great pleasure. But the cat! No!'

He banged his hand on the table.

No one took any notice but a young woman suddenly appeared before them. She was dressed in black and had a dark shawl over her head.

'You are becoming argumentative,' she said to Metaxas. 'It is time for you to go to the hospital.'

14

'Hey! He can't!' cried Seymour. 'He's got a job to do!'

'I know his jobs,' said the woman, standing over them implacably, like some dark figure from Greek tragedy. 'You've been drinking,' she said accusingly. 'Again!'

'I've been having breakfast!'

'And you've been encouraging him,' she said to Seymour.

'No, I haven't!' protested Seymour.

'He is a guest, a colleague!' cried Metaxas. 'Just out from England!'

'Is this true?' she asked Seymour.

'Yes.'

'You're a doctor?' she said. 'Out from England?'

'I'm a policeman.'

'He arrived last night,' said Metaxas. 'I went to the hotel this morning and he hadn't had breakfast. So –'

'So you took him to the Plaza? Well,' she said to Seymour, 'perhaps you really don't know any better. But you do,' she said, turning back to Metaxas.

'Breakfast. That's all it was,' said Seymour, conciliatorily.

'And in England it is the custom to drink ouzo at breakfast?'

'Listen,' said Dr Metaxas, 'I needed a drink before going to the mortuary. That's where the job is.'

'Is this true?' she asked Seymour.

'Yes.'

She thought for a moment, and then nodded.

'All right, then. You'd better go. To the mortuary. *Just* to the mortuary. And then bring him home,' she said to Seymour. '*Straight* home.'

'Are you married?' asked Metaxas.

'No.'

'Take my advice: don't. And if you do, don't have a daughter. Women are always up your tail.'

'Are you going?' she demanded.

'All right, all right,' said Metaxas, getting up.

Arms folded, she watched them set out across the square.

'And you tell your mother I'm bringing a friend home to lunch,' he shot back over his shoulder.

She gave the slightest of nods. Her face, however, remained expressionless. It looked as if it had been carved from marble. And, thought Seymour, rather beautiful.

The cat lay stiffly on the slab. Marble, too. Dr Metaxas bent over it and sniffed. Then he beckoned Seymour forward.

'Smell!' he instructed.

Seymour did so.

'Recognize it?'

Seymour nodded.

'You don't really need anything else,' said Metaxas. 'But we have done everything else. All the usual tests. And for a cat!'

'Have you opened it up?'

'Of course.'

'And found?'

'Traces. Administered in sufficient quantity to cause death.'

'On one occasion?'

'I would say so, yes.'

'Presumably it was with something, or in something?'

'Milk. Again there are traces.'

'What kind of milk?'

'What kind of milk?'

'Goat's, or cow's?'

Metaxas looked at him with a new respect and then turned to one of the white-coated attendants and repeated the question in Greek.

'Cow's,' the man said.

'Isn't that unusual?' asked Seymour, also in Greek. 'In Athens?'

'It is, yes. Mostly we drink goat's milk.'

'I don't know anything about cats,' said Seymour. 'But

16

don't they have a keen sense of smell? Wouldn't the cat have smelt it if it had been put in the milk?'

'It is possible that it was administered with something else that would have disguised the smell,' the man said. 'Marzipan, for instance.'

'Marzipan?'

'We thought we detected traces of marzipan in the bowel contents. The smell would have been not dissimilar, and the taste of the marzipan might have disguised the taste of the other. Especially if the cat was befuddled.'

'Why would it be befuddled?'

'Because it had drunk some alcohol, too.'

Seymour looked at Metaxas.

'Hasn't this cat been living it up a bit?'

Metaxas shrugged.

'It's a royal cat,' he said.

'Any signs of other damage? Wounds, that sort of thing?'

'No,' said Dr Metaxas. 'But every sign of it being pampered, overfed and generally indulged. Whoever killed it was wasting his time. It would have died soon anyway.'

'So,' said Metaxas, as they left the mortuary, 'you speak Greek?'

'Yes.'

'How does that come about?'

'As I told you, I have Greek friends. There are a lot of Greeks in London.'

'There are a lot of Greeks everywhere.'

They walked on in silence. Then Metaxas said:

'You realize that that's what this is all about, don't you?'

'This . . .?'

'All this nonsense about the cat. And the Sultan. And the war.'

'About speaking Greek?'

'And there being Greeks everywhere.'

17

'Why should that lead to –'

'Think of all those Greeks. Scattered everywhere. All round the Mediterranean, in places like Egypt, the Levant, everywhere in the Ottoman Empire. Suppose you could bring them together! Greece would be a great country again. That's what the politicians say, or, at any rate, that's what Venizelos says.'

'Venizelos?'

'Our Prime Minister. It's his "Great Idea". That's what he calls it. He has a dream of the scattered Greeks reunited. Beware of dreams, young man, because they'll lead you astray. They are things of the darkness and they will lead you into the darkness. Venizelos is a good man but he has a dangerous dream. For how are they to be reunited except by war? Great Idea?' He snorted. 'Great Lunacy, I call it!'

They were crossing the square again. He looked at the people sitting at the tables.

'But they like it,' he said. 'The fools! They lap it up like a cat lapping milk from a saucer. A Greater Greece! A return to the old days. What old days? The days of Alexander? But Alexander's been dead for a long time, and he was a Macedonian anyway! But they lap it up. You've seen the flags, the marching? Wave your flags one day and the next march off to kill and be killed. Show the Ottomans that the Greeks are great again! Pah! Fools! Idiots!'

They were passing the café. Metaxas wavered. He looked at his watch.

'Time for an aperitif, I think,' he said, and sat down at a table.

'One only,' stipulated Seymour.

Metaxas gave him an amused look.

'You sound like my daughter,' he said.

The waiter brought two glasses.

Seymour took a little sip and then put the glass down.

'I take it that the Sultan himself has been given a medical examination?' he said. 'In view of his stomach pains?'

'Oh, yes. Several. By an increasing number of eminent specialists. As the findings of each one in turn are challenged. I myself have examined him.'

'And what did you find?'

'A bad case of indigestion. And fear.'

It sounded as if a motor car was approaching. But, wait a minute, there was something funny about it; it sounded as if it was up in the air. Christ, it *was* in the air!

He jumped up. Everyone was standing up excitedly.

The thing suddenly emerged above the top of the buildings.

'It's one of the new Blériot machines!' someone shouted.

Blériot machines! He'd read about them, of course, in the newspapers. Indeed, he could remember the Frenchman's original flight across the Channel three years before. But he had never actually seen one.

It swooped low across the square, so low that he could see a goggled, helmeted figure in the cockpit.

There was a cheer from the people at the tables.

And then it had passed and was disappearing over the roofs of the houses towards the mountains beyond the city.

A babble of excited conversation broke out in the square.

'There!' someone said. 'We've got three now!'

Seymour sat down again.

'It's the latest craze in Athens,' said Dr Metaxas. 'A rich banker bought one for his son. Then his son's friend persuaded *his* father, also rich, to buy one for him. And now, I gather, someone else has been persuaded.'

'They say we're the only city in the world to have three Blériot machines,' said someone proudly.

'Well, we're not likely to have many more,' said Dr Metaxas. 'That's about exhausted the supply of rich fathers in Athens.'

19

'Oh, yes, but the Government's going to buy some for the army. I read it in the newspaper.'

'They say Venizelos himself is behind it.'

'It's coming back!' shouted someone excitedly.

'There's another one!'

'Two of them!'

Despite himself, Seymour couldn't help standing up.

'Perhaps they'll land! In the square! One of them did, you know. The other day. It circled the Acropolis and then flew down the Rue de Stade. And then it landed! Right here in the square!'

The original Blériot machine had, indeed, been joined by another one and they were both coming back over the city.

At the last moment one of the machines, the one they had seen before, peeled away and headed back towards the Acropolis. The other, distinguished by its different markings, plunged low over the square. They could see the pilot clearly. He waved a gloved hand to the people below.

Dr Metaxas, at the table, went still.

'My son,' he said, with a mixture of pride and resignation. And something else, Seymour thought. Was it fear?

Chapter Two

'Your son?' said Seymour. 'But I thought . . .'

'You are wondering if I am one of the rich fathers? Alas, no. But my son is friendly with one of the rich sons. They're in the same class at university. "Has the son got a sister?" I say to him. "Because you'd be doing much better to be spending your time with her."'

He shook his head.

'The trouble about going around with rich people,' he said, 'is that you develop rich tastes. Without having the money to support them.'

It was evidently a sore topic. He shook his head again and contemplated the bottom of his glass. Then, slightly to Seymour's surprise, he got up from the table.

'We'd better be going,' he said. 'My wife will be expecting us.'

They had lunch in the Metaxases' small garden. It was filled almost entirely with trees crammed close together, fig trees, orange trees and olives, but in the middle was a small space where there was a table and some cane chairs. Shade, Seymour guessed, was what they were after, although here and there among the green foliage were spots of colour where Mrs Metaxas had trailed nasturtiums and marigolds.

Mrs Metaxas was there waiting for them. She was tall and striking, like her daughter, but, unlike her, she was blonde and had the high cheekbones and general cast of face of a Slav. She hardly seemed Greek at all. Well, it was possible, thought Seymour. There were plenty of Slavs close at hand. The daughter was much more like the father, dark and quick and intense.

A sixth place had been laid at the table.

'Andreas won't be coming, Mother,' said the daughter.

'No?' Mrs Metaxas was disappointed.

'He's flying,' said Dr Metaxas.

'Again?'

Dr Metaxas shrugged.

'He spends too much time flying,' said Mrs Metaxas, 'when he should be busy with his studies.'

'He doesn't fly *that* much,' said the daughter, rushing to the defence of her brother. 'Only when George lets him.'

'George lets him fly too often,' said Mrs Metaxas. 'He's another one who should be spending more time on his studies. He's not as clever as Andreas is.'

'Andreas is clever enough,' conceded Dr Metaxas. 'At least, as far as passing examinations goes. That's not what worries me. What worries me is what goes along with all this. The cost –'

'All you think about is money!'

'Well, someone in the house has got to! And it certainly won't be Andreas –'

'Look, George is meeting the expenses –'

'Yes, but it can't go on like that, can it? Andreas will have to pay his share.'

'For God's sake!'

'Aphrodite, will you go and fetch the salad, please?' said Mrs Metaxas, intervening hastily.

The daughter got up reluctantly.

'And the retsina!' Dr Metaxas called after her.

'Alexis, you are not to provoke her!'

'Provoke her?' said Dr Metaxas, amazed. 'She's provoking me!'

Aphrodite returned with a bowl of salad.

'Anyway,' she said, as she put it down, 'the costs will be less now. Now that the Government's buying some

Blériots. It has already set up a servicing base and got an English engineer in. We'll be able to make use of it, and it will bring the cost down –'

'We?' said Dr Metaxas. 'You're not in on this too?'

'Well –'

'Aphrodite,' said Mrs Metaxas, laying down her knife and fork, 'I hope you're not thinking of going up in one of these things yourself?'

'Well –'

'I absolutely forbid it!'

'Why?' said Aphrodite.

'Because it's dangerous.'

'Andreas is perfectly sensible –'

'But George isn't! You know he's not. He's too reck-less –'

'Look, I'm not thinking of going up with George –'

'Don't think of going up with anybody!'

Aphrodite concentrated on her salad.

'Actually,' she said, after a moment, 'I've not got to that stage yet. All I was thinking of doing was helping with the servicing.'

'Helping with the servicing?' said Dr Metaxas, stunned. 'Of a machine that's going to fly in the air? That really does reassure me! What the hell do you know about servicing a Blériot?'

'I've been learning. I've been working with George's mechanic –'

'When?' interrupted Dr Metaxas. 'When? When you're supposed to be at classes? Jesus, I spend all my life's savings on sending my children to university and now I learn they don't go anywhere near the place!'

'Don't exaggerate, Alexis!' said Mrs Metaxas.

'I only go to the workshop in the afternoon,' Aphrodite muttered sulkily.

'But that's when you're supposed to be in the labs! I've told you! That sort of thing is absolutely essential if you're going to become a good doctor –'

'As a matter of fact,' said Aphrodite, concentrating hard on her salad, 'I was thinking of changing faculty.'

The Embassy had told him where the Sultan was presently residing and had made him an appointment for five o'clock. It took him most of the rest of the afternoon to get there. The house was on the eastern edge of the city tucked away in a pine wood. It was approached up a long drive. At the entrance to the drive some Greek soldiers, in bright tunics and baggy pantaloons, were standing guard. He showed them the letter he had been given by the Embassy, an authorization from the Greek Government to approach the house, and, after reading it laboriously, they let him through.

Further up the drive was a wooden barrier, manned this time by Ottoman soldiers in large red fezzes.

'Firman?'

Seymour produced the permit that he had been given, signed this time by the Ottoman Government, and, after they had perused it even more laboriously, he was allowed to proceed.

The house was in a courtyard and at its gates some English sailors were standing sentry. Who was guarding whom from whom Seymour was not quite sure.

Inside the house two cavasses, in splendid uniforms, sprang to attention. A man in a dark European-style suit came forward.

'Monsieur Seymour?' he said in faultless French. 'The Acting-Vizier is expecting you.'

He was shown into a large room and settled on some leather cushions spread on the floor. Perfumed sweets were brought and then some coffee. The dark-suited man sat opposite him and made polite conversation. None of it touched on what Seymour had come for. Seymour sat patiently, remembering from a recent visit he had paid to Istanbul that this was how it was done.

After some time an older man, in long, flowing robes,

came into the room. The other man sprang up and introduced them.

'Mr Abd-es-Salaam . . .'

The Acting-Vizier bowed and seated himself on a cushion. More coffee was brought. Mr Abd-es-Salaam questioned him politely about his journey out from London. This, too, Seymour knew, was how it was done.

'And where would you like to begin, Mr Seymour?'

'With the cat, if I may. I wonder if I could speak to someone familiar with its routines? Someone who could tell me, for instance, about how it was fed?'

'You can speak to me.'

'Oh, yes, well, thank you. Actually, I was hoping I could trouble someone less distinguished. Someone, perhaps, who was closer to the actual arrangements –'

'I see to all arrangements.'

'Yes, I'm sure. But you wouldn't do the actual feeding yourself?'

'A slave does that.'

'Of course. I wonder if I could speak to him?'

The Acting-Vizier and the dark-suited man exchanged glances.

'The slave is . . . an occupant of the harem,' said the dark-suited man.

'Yes?'

'And therefore a woman.'

'Oh, I see. There could be difficulties about my speaking to a woman?'

'Yes, that's right. Yes.'

'I'm afraid I do need to speak to her, however.'

The Acting-Vizier and the dark-suited man exchanged glances again.

'It would take too long to fetch a male relative,' said the Acting-Vizier.

'Perhaps Talal?' suggested the younger man diffidently.

'Yes, perhaps it could be through Talal. I will make arrangements.'

25

He went out. A little later the younger man was summoned. He returned with two people, a woman, dark, muffled and veiled, and a middle-aged man.

'You are Talal?'

'Yes.'

As soon as the man spoke, Seymour realized why he was suitable. He was a eunuch.

'And this is . . .?'

'Miriam.'

'And she attends to the cat?'

'She feeds it.'

'And did she feed it the day that –'

'Yes.'

'Can she tell me what she did? Exactly.'

'I fetched the milk from the kitchen –'

'She fetched the milk from the kitchen –'

Seymour had wondered what language was spoken in the harem. Turkish? Arabic? This, though, was different; a Slav language of some sort.

'And?'

'Gave it to the cat.'

'Was it already poured out for her when she got to the kitchen? Or did they pour it out while she was there?'

'It was already poured out. In a special bowl.'

'Which she took . . .?'

'To the harem apartments.'

'Where, exactly?'

'There is a salon.'

'What did she do then? Put it on the floor?'

'Yes.'

'And then?'

'The cat drank it.'

'At once?'

'Yes. I was late, and it was hungry, and –'

'Were you there? Did you actually see . . .?'

There was a little silence.

'Please try to remember exactly. Were you there? All the time?'

26

The woman, behind the veil, seemed agitated.

'Try to remember exactly.'

'I had to go back to Samira,' the woman said in a low voice. 'She had lost a shoe. I had been looking for it. That's why I was late. The moment I got back she called me again.'

'So you didn't see the cat drink the milk? Not actually drink it?'

'I wasn't gone long. Only a minute. The shoe was under the bed.'

'And when you came back, the cat had finished the milk?'

'Yes.'

'Did it seem . . . all right?'

'It was standing . . . stiffly. I thought it looked odd. But I had to take the bowl back to the kitchen, they don't like it if it's left around where people can trip over it.'

'So you took the bowl back to the kitchen?'

'Yes.'

'Did you smell it?'

'Smell?'

'The bowl. When you took it back.'

'No.'

'You didn't notice a peculiar smell?'

'I didn't notice any smell. I – I was hurrying. I just picked up the bowl and ran. I didn't notice – I swear!' she said agitatedly.

'All right, all right. And then you went back? To the harem apartments?'

'Yes.'

'Straight back? You didn't go anywhere else?'

'No.'

'And what did you find when you got back?'

'The cat – it was horrible! It was stretching and writhing. I could see there was something wrong, so I called Leila –'

'Who is Leila?'

'She is another slave. And she came at once but by then it was too late, the cat was already –'

She began to sob.

'It wasn't my fault,' she said tearfully. 'I have already been beaten.'

'Beaten?'

'Because she didn't do what she should have done,' said Talal.

'What should she have done?'

'She should have tasted it before giving it to the cat,' Talal said. 'To see that it was fit.'

The muffled figure withdrew, sobbing. Seymour sat for a moment thinking. Then he said:

'To the kitchens, I think.'

The dark-suited man led him along corridors and then down some steps.

The kitchen was in a large cellar where several men were working. There were two or three ranges, several braziers and a large fire. It was insufferably hot.

'I would like to speak to the man who prepared the milk.'

'Prepared?'

'Poured it into the bowl.'

The dark-suited man spoke to a short, squat older man who appeared to be the senior kitchen servant. Then he turned to Seymour.

'He is not here.'

'Where is he?'

'He has been beaten.'

'I want to speak to him.'

There was a short delay while the man was fetched.

'Is it always the same man?'

The senior servant nodded.

'And what does he do? Just pour?'

'Yes, Effendi.'

'Does he add anything?'

'Add anything?'

'Alcohol, for instance?'

'Effendi, this is a Muslim cat!'

'Maybe, but the hakims say that there was alcohol in the milk.'

'Effendi, the hakims lie! The milk is pure. It has to be. This is His Highness's cat.'

'Where do you get the milk from?'

'It is brought every morning. It has to be fresh.'

'Who brings it?'

'The herdsman.'

'I wish to speak to him.'

'Effendi, he is not here. He lives up in the mountains, where he keeps his cows. He comes in every morning. And then he goes back to his mountains.'

'I will see him tomorrow morning.'

'Effendi, he comes early . . .'

'At about four o'clock,' said the dark-suited man.

'Nevertheless, I will see him.'

A man was carried in and thrown on the floor.

'This is Ahmed. The man who pours the milk.'

'Ahmed?' said Seymour. He spoke in Arabic since that seemed to be the language of the kitchen.

The man lifted his head.

'Ahmed, you pour the milk?'

'To my cost, Effendi, I do.'

'Tell me what you do. Exactly.'

'It is not much, Effendi. I put the ladle into the urn and then empty it into the bowl.'

'The urn is standing where?'

'Over there in the corner, Effendi. Ari brings a new one every morning. It is special milk, Effendi. Cow's, not goat's. The cat would not have any other.'

'Once the milk is in the bowl, where do you put it?'

'Over there, Effendi, on the table. Then it waits until Miriam comes.'

29

'Does anyone go near it?'

'On pain of death, Effendi,' said the senior servant.

'Right. And then Miriam comes in and takes the milk. Where does she taste it?'

'Taste it?'

'I understand that she tastes it before giving it to the cat.'

'It is part of her duties, Effendi.'

'So when does she taste it?'

'When she comes in, Effendi,' said Ahmed, still prone on the floor.

'And did she do that on the morning the cat died?'

'It appears not, Effendi.'

'Appears? But are you sure?'

'Suleiman swears that she did not.'

'Is Suleiman here?'

A man came forward.

'Effendi, every morning she tastes. But that morning she did not. She was late, and came hurrying in, and picked up the bowl and rushed out again. I saw she had not tasted the milk but I thought, what does it matter? We know the milk is the best. And, anyway perhaps she will taste it before she gives it to the cat.'

'Suleiman, did anyone else go to the milk? While it was standing on the table?'

'Oh, no, Effendi. Only Miriam. We must not go near it, lest we spill dirt or grease into it. The milk must be pure, Effendi. Pure for His Highness's cat.'

'Thank you, Suleiman. And thank you, too, Ahmed.'

He was carried away.

'Why was he beaten?' asked Seymour.

The dark-suited man shrugged.

'The milk was to blame,' he said. 'Therefore those who are to do with the milk are also to blame.'

'Next, Leila,' said Seymour.

And with Leila, naturally, Talal. They went through the

same indirect pattern as before. Seymour found it frustrating because he liked to see people's faces as they spoke and make his assessment. Here the witness was doubly removed, by sight and also by language. With the language, though, he could pick up something. In the case of Miriam, the language she and Talal had used had been some kind of Slav tongue, Serbian, possibly. Seymour couldn't speak it but he could speak Russian and Polish so could gather a sense of what she had said without relying wholly on Talal. In the case of Leila, the language was Russian, which he understood much better.

Yes, said Leila, Miriam had called for her. She had just started doing Irina's hair. Before that she had been helping Miriam look for Samira's shoes. Samira had been in a great passion and had had them all joining in the search. But Irina had been getting cross, too, she had been waiting for her hair to be done, so Leila had gone to her. And she had just started when Miriam had called. Leila had known at once that there was something very wrong. Miriam wouldn't have called otherwise. She had left Irina's hair and rushed out to Miriam, still with the brushes in her hands.

And there she had seen the cat. She had seen at once that it was too late to do anything. She had shouted for Talal –

'That is true, Effendi,' said Talal.

– and then there had been a great commotion, but she had had to go back to Irina, if only because Irina had wanted to know what was going on. And then Irina had gone in to see Samira, and they had both summoned Leila and Miriam to give them accounts of what had happened. And then the other wives had wanted to know, and meanwhile the eunuchs were rushing around. And then the Vizier had come, and they had all known that there would be trouble.

And there *was* trouble. First Miriam had been beaten, and then Ahmed. Others had probably been beaten, too, but Leila had not yet heard their names. The Sultan was

31

said to be mad with grief, and Leila could quite believe it, she knew how he had cared for that cat.

All this was poured out in a great flood which taxed Talal's interpreting skills severely. Leila, it appeared, was in a state of great excitement, and so, too, it appeared, was the entire harem. They had talked of nothing else for days, even Irina, who normally had no time for harem gossip. It had all been –

A lot of fun, thought Seymour.

'– absolutely horrible,' said Leila breathlessly.

'Samira,' said Seymour.

The dark-suited man was taken aback.

'The Lady Samira? But she is one of the wives!'

'I won't need her for long.'

'Yes, but –'

The man, perturbed, went off to see the Acting-Vizier. Abd-es-Salaam reflected, and, possibly, checked with His Highness himself, and then agreed. What was one woman among so many? What was a woman, anyway? Set against the background of important issues and events? Whether she was a wife or a slave.

Yes, but . . . how, the man evidently asked? Having already given time to this question, the Acting-Vizier was not inclined to give more time. He had answered it once, the same answer would surely do. Talal.

But Talal as a medium for a servant girl was one thing, the assistant pointed out, Talal as medium for a wife was surely quite another. The Acting-Vizier, who had not made such a difference between the two categories, said that his answer stood. The assistant, who appeared to be a kind of secretary, swallowed and set the process in motion.

And here things began to go wrong. Not a lot happened in the harem and Samira was quite prepared to give interest to her day by answering the tall, handsome Englishman's questions (any man was handsome, after the eunuchs, she told Talal). She readily agreed to the suggested process. She was, or had been once, a Muslim and was, of course, eager to observe the proprieties. A woman could speak to a strange man only in the presence of a male relative or substitute for him, and, lacking anyone else, Talal would do. However, once the questioning had started, Samira took over.

'If I may ask the Lady Samira a few questions . . .' began Seymour.

'Certainly!' said Samira, and then, in excellent French, 'Go ahead.'

'My Lady –' began Talal.

'Shut up.' And then, to Seymour: 'What did you wish to ask me? And how long have you been in Athens? Dreadful place, isn't it? Not like Paris. Now, that's where I would really like to go. Have you been there?'

'I come from London –'

'Not bad. Regent Street is quite good for the shops, I understand, and I would like to ride up the Mall.'

'And have been to Istanbul,' said Seymour desperately.

'Tough. But not in a carriage. At least, not in a closed one. A landau would be better, so that everyone could see me. But actually I wouldn't mind riding on a horse.'

She took a quick look at Seymour to see the effects of her words.

'So that everyone would see you?' said Seymour gamely. 'You would be a sensation.'

'I expect I would. But I couldn't wear trousers. That would be immodest. And a skirt on a horse looks rather silly, don't you think? So it had better be a landau.'

'The cat,' said Seymour doggedly.

'Damn the cat!' said Samira.

'Willingly. But nevertheless there are some questions I have to ask you about it.'

'Oh, very well,' said Samira sulkily. 'Make them short, though, so that we can talk about other things.'

'Lady Samira –' began Talal feebly.

'Shut up. The cat, then. Do we have to?'

'Yes,' said Seymour firmly. 'A distressing occurrence –'

'Not very,' said Samira. 'A damned good job, if you ask me. It tore my stockings once. Good stockings they were, too, from Paris. I'd have killed the brute myself only someone got in ahead of me.'

'It was poisoned. And in the harem.'

'It would have to be in the harem. It never goes anywhere else.'

'Yes, but, you see, that restricts the possibilities for poisoning it. And the people who could have done it.'

'Look, when I said I could have done it, I didn't really mean –'

'No, no, I'm not suggesting that.'

'It could have been anybody. Irina, for instance. She's the sort of ruthless bitch – but it could have been anyone.'

'Exactly. And so I need to know about the precise circumstances. The poison was in the milk the cat was given. The milk was fetched by Miriam, the slave girl –'

'Who should have tasted it,' interrupted Samira. 'I'll bet it was poisoned before it got to the harem.'

'That is a possibility, of course. Alternatively, the poison could have been put in the milk *after* it had got to the harem. Miriam put the bowl on the floor and then you called her – Did you, in fact, call her?'

'Yes.'

'She left the bowl and went to your room. For how long was she with you?'

'Not long. I had lost one of my shoes. *She* had lost one of my shoes. It was a shoe I particularly wanted to put on, it went with the dress I had chosen. And then she couldn't find it! And, do you know what? It was under the bed all the time! The useless bitch! She found it as soon as she really started looking.'

'And that took about how long?'

'Ten minutes? No longer.'

'And then she went back to the cat. By this time it had drunk up all the milk and was already feeling the effects. So it must have been in that time, in those ten minutes, that the poison was put in the milk.'

34

'So it wasn't me, then,' said Samira with relief.

'So who could it have been, then?'

'It couldn't have been Leila, because she was with me. She came to help look for the shoe when Miriam went to the kitchen.'

'There would be others, though?'

'Let me think. It's a sort of puzzle, isn't it? Who could it have been? The wives would have been dressing. Except for Berthe, who would still have been flat on her bum in bed. But everyone else would have been getting up, and their maids would have been with them. It's a busy time, that time in the morning. Everyone's busy.'

'How many wives are there?'

'Six. Here, that is. He only brought six. He had to leave the rest behind.'

'And how many servants?'

'Five women. He should have brought six, one for each. I told Abd-es-Salaam that. But he said he had to cut back and it was either wives or servants, so it was going to be wives.'

'Eunuchs?'

'Three. I said we didn't need them at all, but he said it would be a bad thing if everyone was a woman, you wouldn't know what they were up to.'

'And what would the eunuchs be doing while the wives were dressing?'

'I don't know. What would you be doing, Talal?'

'Having breakfast. And completing my toilette,' said Talal with dignity.

'There you are! The poor dear would be completing his toilette! But you don't need to bother about him. It wouldn't have been any of the eunuchs. It would have been one of the wives. My goodness, how exciting. I'll work out who it was and then let you know. You must come and see me again. Soon. Tomorrow, shall we say? About five in the afternoon. Now let's forget about the cat

35

because there are more interesting things I want to talk to you about . . .'

Talal gave a despairing look off-stage. Someone must have been standing there, probably the Acting-Vizier, for a moment later he came into the room.

'Thank you, Lady Samira. That will be all.'

'We were just getting to the interesting bit,' grumbled Samira.

'No doubt; however, there may be other people that Mr Seymour wishes to see.'

Seymour, still reeling, had his doubts about this. There was something surreal about the whole business of investigating the death of a cat; and what he had seen of the harem so far added to the surreality. However, there was policeman's work to be done, and he grasped for it as a swimmer might grasp for a rock in a stormy sea.

'Yes. Thank you. I do, indeed. The Lady Irina.'

Samira stopped on her way out.

'Yes, that's right. Question the bitch. She would definitely have had something to do with it. And she had never liked that cat.'

'Thank you, Lady Samira.'

She was hustled off.

'My Lord,' said Talal hesitantly, 'do you wish me . . .?'

'Of course. But you'd better try harder this time. You let her do all the talking.'

The eunuch swallowed.

'I do my best, My Lord.'

Another dark, veiled form appeared. This one was taller than the last and, Seymour thought, although you could never quite tell under all the muffle, slimmer.

'My Lady Irina,' said Talal determinedly.

'Thank you, Talal, that will do.'

'But, My Lady —'

'French,' she said to Seymour, 'or Italian? You don't speak Arabic or Turkish, I expect.'

'French,' said Seymour.

'My Lady,' said Talal, 'it is not seemly for a Muslim lady to speak to a man –'

'But I'm not a Muslim lady,' said Irina. 'I'm a Christian.'

'But, My Lady –'

The Acting-Vizier came in.

'It is not seemly for a Royal *wife* to speak to a man *either*,' he said.

'But, Abd-es-Salaam,' cooed Irina, 'I was just trying to be helpful!'

'Let Talal do the talking,' directed the Acting-Vizier, and went out.

Irina came forward and placed herself firmly between Seymour and Talal.

'What was it you were going to ask him to ask me?' she said.

'It is about the cat,' said Seymour.

'Of course. The poor, fat, crazed cat that His Highness so much loved, and that Samira poisoned.'

'I don't think she could have poisoned it, My Lady Irina. She was in another room when the milk was brought in and stayed there, with her servant, Miriam, whom she had called, the whole time the cat was drinking the milk.'

'So?' said Irina. 'She got somebody else to put the poison in the milk. Talal, for instance.'

'I was having my breakfast!'

'So you say!'

'Along with Hassan and Ali. They can prove it.'

'The eunuchs always stick together,' said Irina dismissively.

'It could have been anyone in the harem, My Lady,' said Seymour. 'Yourself, for instance.'

'So it could,' admitted Irina cheerfully. 'Because I went in to see the cat that morning. I was going to pick it up so that I could have it on my lap when His Highness came in so that he could fondle it and not me.'

'You went into the room?'

'That's right.'

'Where the cat was drinking the milk?'

'Yes.'

'You actually saw it?'

'Yes. Only it was spewing it up disgustingly so I thought I would leave it. Let him pick it up, I thought, if it's that messy.'

'And then what?'

'I went back to my room and lay on the divan. And then I heard Miriam shouting, and then Leila, and then one of the eunuchs – was it you, Talal? – and someone said that the cat was a goner, so I thought: That's a relief! and stayed where I was until it had all been cleaned up.'

'Lady Irina, did anyone *see* all this? See you in the room? Or going into the room?'

'How do I know?'

'You might have met someone.'

'Well, I didn't. They were all busy, getting dressed. Or having breakfast,' she shot at Talal.

'At least I can prove it,' said Talal. 'Whereas you, My Lady Irina –'

'Thank you, Talal. That's enough from you. You'd better shut up or else I shall have to poison you too.'

Chapter Three

The next morning Seymour arrived at the Sultan's residence early; so early that the stars were still twinkling in the sky. The house itself could barely be seen in the darkness, and only one Greek guard appeared to be on duty and he didn't seem to be very much on duty, slumped as he was against the small hut which served as guard room. He looked up as Seymour went past, scrambled to his feet, felt for his rifle, which he couldn't find, and said:

'What are you doing?'

'Going to see the Sultan. Here are my papers.'

The guard looked at them uncertainly. Seymour realized that he couldn't read and pointed to the seal.

'Official,' he said. 'The Government seal.'

The guard peered and traced round the embossment with his finger.

'So it is,' he said, surprised, and waved Seymour through.

The Ottoman soldiers, a little along the drive, were crouched around a small camp fire; and remained crouched when Seymour approached. At the last moment one of them opened his eyes.

His cry roused the others. They stood up and thrust at Seymour with their bayonets.

'I've got a firman!' said Seymour hastily.

'Yes, but – It's too early. No one will be up.'

'They are expecting me.'

'Expecting you? At this hour?'

The guards remained doubtful. Then one of them said:

'What are you, then? You don't sound like a Greek.'

'I'm British.'

'Oh, that's all right, then. So long as you're not Greek.'

The French and British guard was not in evidence at all. The gates were closed. Seymour hammered on them and eventually an English sailor appeared.

'What's all this, then?'

'I am expected.'

'Not by us, you're not!'

'Well, I bloody am! Why don't you go in and find out? Seymour, the name is.'

The man went back behind the gates and Seymour heard him say: 'Got a man 'ere –'

'Is 'e the bloody milkman?'

The sailor came out and inspected Seymour.

'Doesn't look like it.'

'He's the one I want to talk to!' said Seymour, exasperated.

'Says 'e wants to talk to the milkman.'

'Oh, yes. Very likely!'

'Why don't you bloody send –'

''E can't be the milkman. The milkman's just bloody coming.'

Up the drive came a small cart.

'I'm from the f—ing Embassy and I've got an appointment!'

''E sounds quite British,' said the sailor doubtfully.

'I f—ing am, and I'll have you hanged from the f—ing yardarm, or wherever they f—ing hang you from, if you don't send in this minute –'

'British,' said the sailor, and went back inside.

Seymour could hear the muttered discussion.

'There'll be no one there.'

'Yes, but 'e says 'e's got an appointment. Get François to stick 'is 'ead in –'

'Christ, there *is* someone there!'

40

'Good morning, Mr Seymour,' said the Acting-Vizier's assistant, coming through the gates.

They followed the milkman's cart round to the back of the house, where the milkman picked up the single urn it was carrying and took it through an open door. They followed him in and found themselves in the kitchen, where several men were already at work.

'Right, Ari, put it down there, will you?' said the senior servant, the one Seymour had spoken to the day before.

The milkman placed the urn carefully on the ground and then prepared to go out.

'One moment, herdsman!' said the Acting-Vizier's assistant. 'This is Seymour Effendi and he has some questions to ask you.'

'Me?' said the milkman, surprised.

'It's about the milk,' said Seymour.

'What's wrong with the milk? It was a bit hot yesterday, that's all it was. It got to the milk. But it's all right today.'

'No, no, I just wanted to know –'

'Listen, the milk's all right. You won't find any better milk. The Vizier himself said so. He went round trying everyone's milk all over the mountains and in the end he chose mine!'

'Yes, yes. I'm sure,' said Seymour soothingly. 'It's just that I wondered if there was any point at which anything could be added –'

'You mean water? Listen, I don't water my milk. Some do, but I don't! The Vizier warned me about that. "The cat likes it creamy," he said, "and that's the way it's got to be." "No matter," I said. "I've got the best grass on the mountain, and there's a heavy dew-fall, see, which makes it rich and luscious."'

'Yes, yes. But could anyone *add* anything on the way here?'

'Listen, I milk my cows early. About two o'clock in the

41

morning. And then I bring it down here. Myself. In my own cart. And no one touches it on the way, and no one *could* touch it because I watch over it like a hawk. That's the way the Vizier wants it, and that's the way it is. Touch my milk?' He snorted. 'I'd like to see anyone try!'

'The Vlachs,' whispered the Vizier's assistant, 'are notoriously belligerent. Always causing trouble.'

'What?' said the herdsman.

'Oh, nothing,' said the Vizier's assistant hastily.

'And he's a Vlach?' Seymour whispered back.

'Anything wrong with that?' demanded the herdsman.

'Certainly not!'

'Oh, all right, then. I'll be on my way.'

As he picked up the empty urn, the senior kitchen servant muttered something to the Vizier's assistant.

'Oh, yes. Herdsman,' he said to the Vlach, 'I don't think we'll be needing any more milk.'

The herdsman put down his urn.

'Not needing . . .?'

'The cat's dead.'

'Dead!'

'Poisoned,' said Seymour. 'That's why I've been asking questions about the milk.'

'Well, I can tell you there's nothing wrong with the milk when it gets here.'

'Nor when it leaves the kitchen,' said the senior kitchen servant swiftly.

'I watch over it like a hawk.'

'And I watch over it, too, like a mother watches over her newborn,' said the senior servant unctuously. 'Until the very moment it leaves the kitchen.'

'It's one of those bitches in the harem!' said the herdsman.

'Do you know, I think he could be right,' said the senior kitchen servant.

'Anyway,' said the Vizier's assistant, 'the cat's dead. So there will be no need for your services. See he's paid!' he ordered the senior servant.

'A lot of bother, that cat!' he muttered to Seymour, as they left the kitchen. He dropped his voice still lower. 'Only don't let anyone know I said that.'

Seymour was inclined to agree with him; and still more inclined by the end of the morning, after he had interviewed the other ladies of the harem and their servants. The ladies were insipid and the servants subdued. Even the excitement of the change in the routine did not inspire the ladies and as one muffled figure gave way to another, and as Talal – waxing in importance now that he was not having to handle Samira and Irina – reproduced one mechanical answer after another, Seymour became increasingly fed up with the whole business.

No one had seen or heard anything. The ladies had all been being dressed, the servants had all been dressing them, and the eunuchs claimed to have been enjoying an evidently interminable breakfast. Certainly – or so they claimed – no one had seen Irina enter the room where the cat had been. Equally, no one had seen anyone approach the bowl in the time between Miriam's putting it down and her return to find a stiffening cat.

Seymour tried to check alibis but found it difficult. Unable to see the faces of the ladies, he couldn't get a sense of whether they were telling the truth or not. When he tried to test one account against another, he found that the ladies all hung together like glue. The eunuchs, polite in the extreme, warily confirmed each other and their general absence from the scene. Only the servant maids showed occasional flashes of independent life, and these were hard to detect behind the dark drapes and the long veils which went from head to toe.

By the end of the morning Seymour had got nowhere; and the only thing that was clear in his mind was that if he had been in the harem he would probably have taken a pot-shot at the cat himself.

He had been invited to the Embassy for lunch but when he got there he found them having a meeting. A cavass went in to whisper that he had arrived and shortly afterwards the Second Secretary came out to invite him to join them.

They had obviously been discussing the situation with respect to the ex-Sultan. After he had been sitting there for a few minutes Seymour thought he had worked out who they were. There was a senior representative of the Greek Government and also an Ottoman representative, from, it appeared, a neighbouring Ottoman administration. Salonica, that was it. The British Embassy was, of course, well represented – the First Secretary was in the chair – and so was the French Embassy. There were also various people whom he couldn't quite make out but suspected to be interested parties from countries round about.

'Perhaps it would be helpful if Mr Seymour could give us his impressions,' said the First Secretary.

'Well, of course, they're first impressions only but at the moment I'm inclined to believe that the cat's death – which is what you've asked me to investigate – is something to do with a harem squabble, merely a by-product of a quarrel between the wives.'

It didn't go down well.

The senior French representative frowned.

'No, no,' he said, 'you haven't got the picture.'

'It is early days yet,' said the Greek representative genially, 'and Mr Seymour has not yet had time to penetrate through the murk. But when he has, he will find that there is a political dimension.'

'He certainly will,' said the Ottoman representative, 'and that most of the politics are directed at the person of His Esteemed Highness, Abdul Hamid.'

'Not so esteemed,' retorted the Greek representative. 'You threw him out.'

'He stepped aside,' said the Ottoman representative loftily, 'in the interests of peace.'

'Peace is in everyone's interests,' said the First Secretary. 'It is what we all want.'

'It's not what the Greeks want,' said the Ottoman representative. 'They want war. And they are prepared to murder the Sultan Abdul Hamid in order to get it.'

'If anyone murders Abdul Hamid,' responded the Greek representative, 'it will be the Ottomans. They want to get rid of him, and they want it to look as if we did it!'

'Gentlemen, gentlemen!' said the First Secretary. 'I thought we were all agreed that these dark suspicions must be carefully looked into. And that is exactly what Mr Seymour has started to do.'

'He hasn't got very far yet.'

'He has allowed the wool to be pulled over his eyes.'

'Naive!'

'He has made a start,' said the First Secretary patiently.

'Start, pooh!' said one of the interested parties. Macedonian, perhaps? 'He had better get on with it. Anyone can see what is building up. First, the cat, then the Sultan. And then war.'

'It must stop at the cat,' said the French representative.

'Mr Seymour, I am sure, will see that it does.'

'Maybe,' said the Greek representative. 'But, just to be sure, we are putting an extra guard around the Sultan.'

'Of Greeks? That will fill everyone with confidence!' said the Ottoman representative sarcastically. 'I am afraid that in that case we will have to put an extra guard around the Sultan, too.'

The French and the British members looked at each other.

'I am afraid that is not very satisfactory,' said the First Secretary.

'No,' said the senior French representative. 'I am sorry,

45

but we shall have to insist that there be an independent international guard too.'

'Why?' said the Greek representative. 'I must protest! This is Greek territory!'

'Temporarily,' said the Ottoman representative. 'And I must point out that the Sublime Porte has consistently argued that Greece is still part of the Ottoman Empire!'

'It is for these reasons,' said the French representative, 'that an international guard is necessary.'

The Second Secretary, sitting on Seymour's right, passed a slip of paper to the First Secretary, on Seymour's left. As it passed, Seymour read it: 'Lunch,' it said.

The First Secretary began to gather up his papers.

'We are agreed, then? Good! I think I can say that the Sultan's life is precious to all of us.'

Seymour had had much to do with politics. He was in the Special Branch of the Criminal Investigation Department at Scotland Yard and his work in the East End was almost exclusively on the political side. That is to say, it was concerned with the revolutionaries, anarchists, terrorists and political activists who, in the opinion of the newspapers, constituted the bulk of the immigrant population of East London. In Seymour's experience it wasn't quite like that but the newspapers persuaded the politicians and the politicians persuaded the police and the police, anyway, it sometimes seemed to Seymour, persuaded themselves and there certainly were lots of nutty, although on the whole pacific, people in the areas he worked in, who kept him happily occupied. He found himself developing quite an affection for the dirty underworld of politics. He found, too, as his duties began to draw him occasionally abroad, that his experience of domestic politics gave him considerable insight into the great world of international politics: although the domestic politics he had in mind was not that of the unfortunate sub-groups of the immigrant East End but that of Whitechapel police

46

station, Special Branch versus the others in Scotland Yard, and Scotland Yard versus the Home Office and the Government generally.

As he matured, or, as his sister put it, his nasty work turned him nastier, he began to develop a political sense of his own. He could see the internal politics in most places.

And certainly in the harem. But the politics he could see there didn't seem to tie up at all with the sort of politics that these blokes seemed bothered about. War? They must be joking. But the Greek representative and the Ottoman representative hadn't seemed to be joking.

'You know,' he said hesitantly to the Second Secretary, as they walked along the corridor together, 'I'm really not convinced that the cat's death *was* political. Not in your sense of the word, at any rate.'

The Second Secretary stopped.

'Listen,' he said, 'in the Balkans *everything* is political.'

At lunch he found himself sitting opposite another Englishman, who had, apparently, arrived in Athens only a few weeks before. His name was Stevens and he was an engineer.

'Aeroplanes,' he said to Seymour.

'Ah, yes. The new Blériot machines. I saw two of them yesterday.'

'Blériot machines?' said the First Secretary. 'I wouldn't have thought there was enough work to keep you going, Mr Stevens.'

'The Government's ordering three,' said Stevens, 'and it'll be my job to service them. I'll have to build up servicing facilities. Because there could be more.'

'More?' said the First Secretary. 'What on earth would they want more for?'

'The war,' said Stevens. 'If it comes.'

The First Secretary looked at his plate.

'Ah, yes,' he said. 'The war.'

'But I still don't see –' said the Second Secretary. 'I mean – what *use* would they be?'

Stevens put down his knife and fork.

'What *use* would they be?' he said incredulously. 'Why, they would make all the difference. Look, suppose you've got mountains, right? As you have in Greece. Lots of them. And there's an army on one side of the mountain and an army on the other. The one that's got Blériots would be able to know what the other was doing.'

'Yes, but you could send someone to take a look, couldn't you?'

'In any case, Mr Stevens,' said the First Secretary, smiling, 'this is Greece. Everyone knows what everyone else is doing.'

'Yes, but you'd know it much more quickly,' said Stevens. 'And if you sent someone on foot, the army could have moved by the time they get back and reported.'

'Armies have managed all right so far,' said the Second Secretary.

'But *have* they managed all right? This would *improve* things. The generals would have more information.'

'Would that improve things?'

'And in any case,' said Stevens earnestly, 'it's not just information. You could drop things.'

'Bricks and things, you mean? But wouldn't that be dangerous? You might hit someone –'

'Bombs,' said Stevens.

'Bombs!' said the First Secretary, aghast.

'I don't think that's very sporting,' said the Second Secretary.

'It's the way it's going to be,' said Stevens.

'But that's – that's terrible! It would transform –'

'Exactly,' said Stevens, picking up his knife and fork again and plying them with relish.

'Have you come across a Miss Metaxas?' asked Seymour,

some time later. 'I gather she's interested in – what was it that you called it? – servicing Blériot machines.'

'Oh, yes. But that's the private machines. I've seen her with the mechanics. You don't often see a woman – but she's quite good. For a woman, I mean.'

'She works as a *mechanic*?' said the First Secretary.

'That's right, yes,' said Stevens. 'On the private machines. There are three of them. That's a lot, you know. For a place like Athens. I've met the people who fly them, too. They're amateurs, of course. But good. They could come in handy if it really does get to war. They'd need training, of course, but with experience, they could be really something. There's a lot of dash about them.'

'We're trying to see that it doesn't get to war,' said the First Secretary.

Stevens shrugged. 'Well, good luck. But from what I can see, over at the army base where I've got my workshop, they're taking it for granted.' He looked at the First Secretary. 'You know, you want to get in on this.'

'The last thing I have in mind!' said the First Secretary.

'No, no, from the country's point of view. England . . . I mean. There's money in it. For British industry, I mean. And it would bring the industry on. A few big contracts would do wonders. And I could help, you know. I'm well placed. I could push things our way. You want to think about it.'

Seymour walked back to the Sultan's residence through a deserted Athens. Everyone was indoors retreating from the heat. In the main square the tables were empty and the cabs had come to a halt. Their drivers were sleeping inside their cabs or else were stretched out in the shade between the wheels. The sunlight was blinding on the new white marble of the buildings. In the drive leading up to the house the guards were once more asleep. They barely looked up at him as he passed.

He had half expected to find the Acting-Vizier's assistant asleep too but he appeared at once.

'Certainly!' he said, and led Seymour to the dark room with the cushions that he had been in before, which obviously served as a reception room. 'What is it that you would like to know?'

'I would like you to tell me about the harem – how it is organized, who runs it, who controls access to it, that sort of thing.'

'Well, of course, it is a very much reduced harem compared with what it was in Istanbul. In Istanbul there were over a hundred wives and many concubines as well. And many servants. The harem spread over several buildings. But when His Highness was . . . obliged to leave he was not able to bring them all with him. The space . . .'

He frowned.

'When we were in Salonica we had more space. That was where we were moved to first. It is, in fact, in Ottoman territory and the Sultan was treated with proper respect. Even though . . . circumstances had changed.'

'Why did he move to Athens?'

'He was worried about his health. The move was not – is not – intended to be anything other than temporary. There are better medical facilities here. And he felt . . . nervous about being treated in Salonica.'

'I see. And what – in general terms, if you like – was the nature of his problem?'

The assistant hesitated.

'It was hard to establish. That, roughly, was why we came to Athens.'

'And then the cat died –'

'Which naturally gave a focus to his worries.'

'Now, of course, the place the cat died was the harem.'

'Yes. You were asking me how it was organized. There are six royal wives – here, that is – each of whom has her own room. It was difficult to find a house with a sufficient number of rooms. The rooms had to be exactly equal, you see, or it would cause trouble. We had to have alterations made. For example, the Sultan's own apartments are actually outside the harem and we had to have a communicating door put in –'

'Doesn't that create a security problem? I understood that access to the harem was strictly controlled?'

'It is. The communicating door is kept locked and only the Sultan has a key.'

'I see. And the six rooms where the wives are, are they kept locked too?'

'Only when the Sultan is inside. Otherwise they are kept not just unlocked but open.'

'Open?'

'The doors are always kept open. There is a degree of . . . what shall I say, invigilation in the harem.'

'And that is the function of the eunuchs?'

'Largely, yes.'

'And they report to . . .?'

'Abd-es-Salaam. The Acting-Vizier.'

'Is there a Chief Eunuch?'

The Vizier's assistant hesitated.

'Ali is the senior eunuch. But there is not yet a Chief Eunuch as there was in Istanbul. The situation is . . . rather fluid. In Istanbul everything to do with the harem was handled by the senior royal wife and the Chief Eunuch. But the senior wife died just before the . . . changes, and the Chief Eunuch was . . .'

'Deposed?'

'Translated to higher things. In Paradise. So the structure of the harem is somewhat undetermined. Especially with respect to the senior royal wife.'

'And who is the senior royal wife?'

'That is the principal thing undetermined. There are two claimants.'

'Samira and Irina?'

'That is right, yes. Normally there is no problem about deciding who is the senior. It is the one who is mother of

51

the Sultan's heir. But the mothers have all been left behind in Istanbul and none of the wives here is yet a mother.'

'So Samira and Irina are fighting it out?'

'The question is not yet resolved,' said the Vizier's assistant evasively.

Afterwards Seymour went down to the kitchens. He found the kitchen servants just getting up from their siesta. They came crawling out from under the tables and under the counters, from behind the strings of onions, peppers, aubergines and garlic that hung from hooks in the ceiling making little private alcoves where people could rest in peace, and from unlikely nooks such as below the sinks. The senior servant was not among them. He was a privileged man and went home to his wife for a couple of hours after lunch. Seymour was pleased. It meant the men might talk more freely.

'I'm glad I didn't come earlier,' said Seymour apologetically. 'I wouldn't have wanted to disturb you.'

'You haven't disturbed us,' they said amicably.

'And I don't want to get in your way if you're busy.'

'Oh, we're not busy,' one of them assured him, putting a large black kettle on the stove.

'It's a slack time for us until we start on the evening meal,' another explained: which was what he had counted on.

'I expect you need a bit of that,' said Seymour.

'We do, we do.'

'I mean, you've got to feed the whole household: the Vizier, the servants, the harem, the Sultan himself, I expect.'

'That's right.'

'That's a lot of food. And then how do you get it round to them? There must be a lot of coming and going. It'll be like a madhouse here at certain times of the day.'

'It is at *all* times of the day,' said someone, grinning.

'What do they do? Send servants to collect it?'

'Some of them do.'

'The harem would have to, wouldn't it? I mean, you couldn't have any old servant going there.'

'No, no.'

'They'd have to be women, for a start.'

'That's right.'

'Do they send the maids along? The ones who wait on the wives?'

'Heavens, no! They wouldn't dirty their hands with anything like that. No, there's an old servant, Amina, her name is, who takes the food.'

'Just the one servant?'

'Well, call it one and a half. She's got a girl, Chloe, who helps her.'

'Does all the work,' said someone. 'Amina mostly sits on her ass.'

'I wonder that they brought her.'

'Had to. She's been with the harem for a long time and knows too much. They didn't want to leave her behind in case she started talking to people.'

'Which she is prone to do.'

Seymour laughed.

'And there'd be plenty to tell, I expect,' he said.

'There would!'

'They get up to it, do they?'

'They'd like to. But it's not so easy. Abd-es-Salaam keeps an eye on them. And then there are those eunuchs, with nothing to do except watch over the women.'

'But I'll bet they'd like to,' said Seymour. 'Locked up in there.'

'Well, there you are.'

'Ever tried it yourselves?'

'What, with the wives? Not a chance!'

'Too risky. He'd have your balls off in a flash.'

'All right, not the wives, then. But how about the slave girls?'

'You might get somewhere with them,' the man conceded. 'But it wouldn't be easy. Not with the eunuchs

53

watching. And the wives would be looking out for it, too. They wouldn't want them to be having something that they were not.'

'Hard to get at them, is it?'

'You could say that.'

'There's easier stuff around,' said someone else.

As Seymour left the kitchen, the Vizier's assistant fell in beside him. Invigilation was not confined to the harem, he realized.

'You have been checking the milk again?'

'I think the milk was pure when it arrived here,' said Seymour. 'Whatever was added, was added either in the kitchen or in the harem.'

The Vizier's assistant nodded.

'It is a pity that that girl didn't taste it, as she was supposed to.'

'Quite a lot was added to the milk,' said Seymour, 'apart from the poison. If the doctors in the laboratory are right.'

'Yes?'

'Marzipan. Or something like it. To disguise the taste. And alcohol.'

'Alcohol!'

'To befuddle the cat.'

The Vizier's assistant was silent for a moment, thinking.

'Wouldn't the alcohol take time to work?'

'It would.'

'And doesn't that mean that it was given to the cat earlier? Before the poison?'

'It might.'

The young man thought.

'And wouldn't that mean that it was administered in the harem? Not the kitchen? And before the milk was fetched?'

'There is another question,' said Seymour.

'Yes?'

'It applies to both the alcohol and the poison. If they were administered in the harem, how did they get into the harem? With all the . . . invigilation.'

Seymour had wanted to speak to Amina, the servant who delivered the food to the harem, but she was nowhere to be found. The Vizier's assistant, whose name, he said, was Orhan Eser, conducted a search for her, with growing exasperation.

'Amina is becoming impossible!' he said.

He hauled out a terrified little girl, who, it appeared, helped Amina to deliver the food.

'Where is Amina?' he demanded.

The little girl was tongue-tied.

'Is she sleeping?'

The little girl managed to nod.

'She does a lot of sleeping these days,' she whispered.

'And where is she likely to be sleeping?'

'She will beat me if I tell,' said the little girl.

'And I will certainly beat you if you don't tell!'

The little girl looked at him with horrified eyes.

'Come, where is she?'

'She sometimes sleeps in the broom cupboard.'

'Show me!'

But Amina was not there.

If the Vizier's assistant had not been a devout Muslim, he would have sworn.

'Leave it till tomorrow,' said Seymour, 'and let me have a word with her then.'

Chapter Four

The next morning when Seymour arrived, Amina was waiting for him, with the Vizier's assistant standing grimly over her. Harem rules did not apply to her but the general Muslim rule that a woman should speak to a man only in the presence of a male relative did. Orhan Eser, however, was having no nonsense this time. He would do, he said firmly: and Seymour suspected that enough conversation had gone on before he arrived for Amina not to demur. She stood meekly before them, a small, bent figure dressed entirely in black, with a headdress completely concealing her face and falling right down to her waist.

Orhan Eser volunteered, too, to interpret, and Seymour was not unhappy about this. They spoke in Turkish and Seymour had enough Turkish to be able to monitor the conversation a little: although he did not tell Orhan Eser this.

'It's about the cat,' Orhan Eser said to Amina.

'I didn't do it!'

'No one's saying that you did. We just want to know some things.'

'I don't know anything about it!'

'The things are general,' said Orhan Eser.

'You deliver the food to the harem?'

'She delivers the food to the harem,' said Orhan Eser.

'And do you go right into the harem?'

Definitely not.

'You give it to the eunuchs at the door?'

A nod of the head.

'Always to the eunuchs? Do you ever give it directly to the waiting ladies?'

Never.

'And does she ever speak to them?'

Never.

'Never?' said Seymour sceptically.

To his credit, Orhan Eser was able to inject the scepticism, and invest it, too, with a degree of threat, which clearly made an impression.

'Occasionally.'

'What about?'

There was a lengthy exchange between Orhan Eser and the old woman.

'A degree of badinage sometimes takes place,' said Orhan Eser stiffly.

'And what about the royal ladies? Does she ever speak with them?'

Never.

'Never?'

Well, very occasionally.

Could she give an example?

She certainly could. At length. A couple of weeks ago the food had been cold. And the Lady Samira had come down and berated everybody: the eunuchs, the kitchen, Amina, although it was not her fault, she was merely – et cetera, et cetera.

'So it does happen that she sometimes speaks to them?'

Not exactly.

What, then?

'They speak to her. She would never presume –' et cetera, et cetera.

'And do they ever ask her to do things for them?'

Do things?

Well, like take a message for them.

Much agitation. Never, never would Amina do such a thing. She knew her place, she had always been loyal to the Sultan, served him for forty years, all of it in the harem, and no one had ever suggested –

And did things ever pass the other way? Go into the harem?

'Gifts, say?'

Amina did not think so. His Highness no doubt lavished gifts on his favourites, but she knew nothing about that.

Or, said Seymour, medicine?

Ah, well, said Amina, suddenly growing garrulous, that was a different matter. Sometimes, occasionally, when they had a headache. Or at a certain time of the month. Or when one of the ladies was suffering from constipation. That was only reasonable, Amina herself suffered from constipation, and –

And love potions.

'What?' said Orhan Eser.

Love potions. Amina's voice changed and became, if that was possible, almost a smirk.

'But – but –' said Orhan Eser, and Seymour was following the Turkish perfectly. 'Who for?'

Amina, presuming on her standing as an old servant and going well beyond the bounds of permissible familiarity, gave him a nudge.

'Why, His Highness, of course!'

'The Sultan?'

'To pep him up.'

'Amina –'

'They all do it. All the wives when they think it's going to be their turn. Priming the pump, so to speak!' she cackled.

'That will do, Amina!'

'Although they say he doesn't need it!'

'Enough!'

Amina went off, still cackling.

It was with some relief that Seymour was able to put his questions directly and not through an intermediary. All the eunuchs spoke French and one, even, English, although he was more at home in French and Seymour conducted the conversation in that language. They all swore that nothing passed into or out of the harem, nothing at all.

Food? Well, of course food. They had to eat, didn't they?

What happened when the food was brought? Did they take it from Amina with their own hands?

Well, not exactly. One of them stood by the door and watched Amina give it to the maids, who distributed it around the harem. It was not for them, superior creatures as the eunuchs were, to do such menial tasks themselves. As is the way with superiors all over the world, they preferred to watch others do it. And that, in any case, was their job: to watch, and see that nothing untoward occurred.

And what happened afterwards? When the dishes were removed.

The maids placed them at the door.

And then?

The door was opened and they were taken away.

By Amina?

Not always by Amina. Usually she left it to the little girl who worked with her, Chloe, her name was. Amina, too, in her way, was a superior person and did not deign to bother herself with dirty dishes.

The door was opened, then: who by?

The eunuch on duty.

And did he have speech with Chloe?

He might let drop a word, but Chloe was really too low in the pecking order to be worth exchanging many words with.

Nevertheless, the maids? Did they ever have a chance to enter into conversation at the door?

Well, they might – he knew what women were. But the eunuch on duty wouldn't let them talk too long, they had work to do, and the royal wives would be angry if they summoned a maid and she wasn't immediately available.

What about the royal wives themselves? Did they ever come to the door?

No. Well, the Lady Irina had come to the door recently to complain about a crack in one of the plates. She had pointed it out to the eunuch, and the eunuch had pointed it out to Chloe, and Chloe had dissolved into tears, and the eunuch had said she was a silly girl, and the Lady Irina had got into a temper and said that it was nothing to do with Chloe, it was for the eunuch to sort out. She had spoken very intemperately to the eunuch and he had been very much hurt. He would have complained, but there was no one at the moment for him to complain to. He had mentioned it to Ali, and Ali had remonstrated with the Lady Irina, but she had told him to piss off, which was not a seemly thing for a royal wife to say, and the wives were beginning to get out of hand and His Highness should do something about it –

Okay, okay. Leave the food. Does anything else go into the harem? Medicine, for instance? He had heard that medicine sometimes passed into the harem.

Well, of course, if the doctor prescribed it. There had been a lot of doctors lately, usually to see His Highness, of course. But sometimes while they were there the royal ladies sought to take advantage of it and called them in –

Into the harem?

No, no. The wife would be taken out of the harem and put in a separate room, behind a screen, and the doctor could talk to her there.

With a eunuch present?

Of course.

Seymour asked if he could have the doctors' names. There were twelve of them.

'Just the ones called into the harem, please.'

That reduced the list to five: an eminent Italian specialist who had since returned to Rome, an equally eminent (although this was disputed by the Greeks) specialist from

Istanbul who had been visiting relatives in Salonica, and who had returned to that city, a Frenchman working in Athens, and two Greeks. The second Greek name on the list was that of Dr Metaxas.

Seymour went to see the other Greek and the Frenchman that afternoon. They had both prescribed medicines for ladies of the harem, the Frenchman a purgative, the Greek a sedative. Neither had thought their patients in any danger, or indeed, ill.

'Nerves,' said the Greek specialist.

'Biliousness,' said the Frenchman.

And the cat, said Seymour; had they been called on to prescribe anything for the cat?

They both looked at him strangely.

He had arranged to meet Samira at five o'clock. Or, rather, she had arranged to meet him. *Could* she do that? With all these restrictions on access to the harem and the 'degree of invigilation' that prevailed? He had assumed that the ladies of the harem were totally controlled, suppressed, supine, unable to take any initiative whatsoever. Admittedly, Samira and Irina could hardly be described as subdued but the impression he had of the others was that subjugation had drained away all capacity of initiative, leaving them inert and resigned to their lot, content to stay within the rules laid down for them.

But could the rules be bent? It seemed so, if Samira could indeed override the system. And at first it looked as if she could. Just before five Seymour was hanging around, not exactly expecting to see her but anxious not to lose the opportunity if he could, when along came Talal, the eunuch. Seymour learned later that the time of five o'clock was not casually chosen. It was when Orhan, the Vizier's assistant, was still at his rest and supervision left to the eunuchs, who were more subject to being overborne.

He led Seymour into a small room off one of the inner corridors, dark – lit by only a single, beautiful, old oil lamp – and with rich carpets on the walls and soft cushions on the floor. On one of these the Lady Samira was sitting impatiently.

'At last we are alone!' she said. 'Apart from Talal, Ali and Hassan.'

'That was the condition,' murmured Talal imperturbably.

'And we are to remain at arm's length.'

'*Two* arms' length!'

'Well, of course, I may define that in a way very different from yours.'

'We are going by my definition,' said Talal.

'Perhaps we can relax the conditions at future meetings,' said Samira. 'Because there will have to be a lot of meetings if I am going to tell Mr Seymour all the things that I find out. Because I shall be working hard on this, as I really want to find out who killed that rotten cat, especially if it was Irina.'

'You have ten minutes, My Lady Samira.'

'Thank you, Talal. I know I can count on you to remind me of anything that is unpleasant. But you are right, Talal: time is pressing, and Mr Seymour waits.'

'I am, naturally, very interested to hear what you have to tell me, Lady Samira.'

'I am sure you are. But let us, for the moment, get back to the cat. The key thing, it seems to me, is who was free and unobserved between the moment when Miriam left the bowl and the moment some time later when she went back to find the cat already stricken. We can narrow it down a little. The poison would have taken some time to work so it was probably put in the milk very soon after Miriam left. Furthermore, the cat was not waiting greedily in the room when Miriam put down the bowl, as it normally is, but slumped on a cushion in the neighbouring room, where Irina was stuffing it with chocolates.'

'My Lady Samira, are you sure about this? Because it does not quite correspond to what the Lady Irina told me.'

'Look, if you are expecting any correspondence between what the Lady Irina tells you and the truth, then you are totally misguided.'

'But are you certain that she was in the adjoining room, and with the cat?'

'Certainly, Zenobia saw her.'

'And she was feeding the cat sweets?'

'Stuffing the brute.'

'With chocolates, did you say?'

'She had gone through boxes of them.'

'And . . . did any of the chocolates contain marzipan?'

'Marzipan?'

'Could you check that for me?'

'I certainly could.'

'Lady Samira,' interposed Talal, 'would you kindly observe the "arm's length" condition.'

'I am.'

'You're not. You've moved closer.'

'That is so that Mr Seymour can *hear*.'

'He can hear perfectly well.'

'He can't. Can you, Mr Seymour?'

'What? Excuse me –'

'You see? He can't hear.'

'That is because you've dropped your voice.'

'I have a sore throat. It may be that my voice fades occasionally. So, out of courtesy to Mr Seymour, I lean close –'

'Your ten minutes is up.'

'Look, you can see how important Mr Seymour thinks what I have to tell him is.'

'You can tell him next time.'

'Talal, I am doing this for the Sultan. He is *very anxious* to find out who killed the cat. And Mr Seymour is helping him. And I am helping Mr Seymour. And you, Talal, are not helping at all.'

'Ten minutes! Up!'

Samira got to her feet unwillingly. Then, before Talal could stop her, she walked over to Seymour and put out her hand.

'Until we meet again,' she breathed.

'Lady Samira, this is indecent!'

As Seymour was walking along Stadion Street he heard himself hailed from a passing carriage. It was Aphrodite Metaxas. The carriage pulled into the side of the road beside him. It was one of the little, open, four-seater ones, with, for some reason which he was never able to establish, the British coat of arms painted on the doors.

'Are you going our way?'

'I'm going to Constitution Square.'

'Get in.'

He climbed up and sat down beside her.

'You know about these carriages? They're like taxis. You pay ten lepta a seat. You only find them in Stadion Street, but they're handy for me coming from the School of Medicine.'

'You've been in the lab this afternoon, have you? Not working on the Blériot?'

'Yes, I'm there most afternoons, actually. I only told my father I was in the workshop so as to provoke him.'

'And are you really thinking of changing faculty?'

'Not really. There's not much working on actual engines in the engineering faculty of Athens University, I can tell you! And my father would be so disappointed. He's set his heart on me becoming a doctor. Why, I ask him? Doctors are two-a-penny in Athens. Listen, he says, you've got to think of your future. What happens after I am gone? Oh, I'll marry some rich man, I say. You'll be lucky, he says: rich men can afford to be discriminating. Anyway, I say, there'll be more money in becoming a Blériot mechanic than in becoming a doctor. They're in much shorter supply. And they'll be greatly in demand when the war comes and we get more machines. No, they won't, he says, not after

64

the machines have crashed. Which they're pretty likely to do if you're the one who is servicing them.'

She laughed, then sobered up.

'Actually, my mother doesn't like that kind of talk. And she likes it still less now that Andreas is getting –'

She broke off.

'Getting?'

'Getting involved, you might say. Certainly he's very excited. All the young men are. My father gets very angry. he says that war is stupid. The rush of the Gadarene swine, he says. And my mother says it's immoral.'

'And what do you say?'

She shrugged.

'I don't know,' she said. 'It's both, of course: stupid and immoral. But maybe it's inevitable. That's what everyone is coming to feel. My father says it's the politicians. You know, Venizelos and his "Great Idea". He says it would be a greater one if Venizelos led us in exactly the opposite direction. But the politicians are leading us all astray, he says. Especially the young, who don't know any better. He says.

'I'm not sure about that. There's a lot of talk about it at the university, with people arguing on both sides. But my brother, Andreas, isn't really interested in all that, the ideas, I mean. He's just – excited. They all are, all the aviators – that's what we call the ones that fly. They've taken to going over to the army base every afternoon. There's a new man there who knows a lot about flying machines, an Englishman, an engineer, named Stevens. They talk a lot to him and he says that war would be a great opportunity for aviation. It would bring it on immensely, it always does. It would make aviation really big, he says, and that would change the world.

'It seems unlikely to me. But he's very enthusiastic and they listen to him. It appeals to them, both as young men and as flying men. And it does to Andreas, too. He see himself as a sort of flying hero.

'It makes my father very angry. "You see yourself as a

65

flying Hercules," he says. "But remember the story of Daedalus and Icarus. Daedalus built wings so that man could fly. And he went up with his son, Icarus, to show them. But they flew too near the sun and the wax holding the wings on melted. Icarus fell into the sea and was drowned. And Daedalus, who had thought it all up, landed safely. Venizelos will be like Daedalus and land safely. But you bloody won't." Says my father.'

When they reached Constitution Square, the carriage stopped and everyone got out.

'I am going to find my father,' said Aphrodite. 'Why don't you come with me? He will be glad of masculine reinforcement.'

The square was now full of people. Every table outside the cafés was occupied and often there were people standing beside them chatting. Everyone was chatting. The cab drivers dismounted from their carriages to join in the general conversation. Around each cab a small group, usually of men, was gathered. In the middle of the square, with total disregard for any cart or carriage that might be passing, people walked to and fro: chatting.

Old Tsakatellis, back in London, had said something about this, too.

'The Greeks,' he said, 'love to talk. Everyone has an opinion and wants to express it. That is the basis of democracy.'

'Yes,' said Dr Metaxas, when Seymour put this view to him, 'but the trouble is, it's just talk. They never *do* anything.'

They found him sitting at a table with some friends.

'My God!' he said, looking up. 'What is this: a posse? The police as well? That, surely, Aphrodite, is unnecessary: I'll come quietly!'

66

Aphrodite was shaking hands with the other people around the table. Evidently she knew them all.

'It's all right, Aphrodite!' one of them said. 'We were just throwing him out!'

'A likely story!' said Aphrodite.

'It's true, though. We're supposed to be meeting some friends.'

One of them glanced at his watch.

'Supposed to have met some friends,' he amended. 'A quarter of an hour ago!'

They hurried away.

Dr Metaxas stayed put.

'I don't suppose I can persuade you . . .' he said.

Aphrodite relented.

'This once,' she said. 'Since you have a friend from England.'

'I regard myself as in custody,' said Dr Metaxas.

He asked how Seymour had been getting on. Seymour told him about the harem.

Aphrodite frowned.

'I don't like these Eastern practices,' she said.

'Well, they're not exactly catching on,' said Dr Metaxas.

'No, but I don't like them,' said Aphrodite. 'It's the disregard for women that I can't stand. One thing I will say for you, Father, is that you brought me up to be equal with men.'

'No, I didn't,' said Dr Metaxas. 'You forced it on me. You and your mother.' He sighed. 'Why did the Greeks have to become independent? Why didn't we stick to the good old Ottoman ways? When man was king, there was no dispute in the house, and everything ran perfectly.'

'For men,' said Aphrodite.

'True. And now nothing runs perfectly for anybody. Well, that, too, is democracy.'

'You will be pleased to know,' said Seymour, 'that, in one respect at least, Aphrodite has been listening to your words. She spent the afternoon at the lab.'

'Did she?'

Dr Metaxas turned to her with some surprise. He asked her what she had been doing and the two had a little, informed discussion of that part of the syllabus. Seymour's attention drifted away.

But suddenly came back again.

'Those are shots!'

'Yes,' said Dr Metaxas.

'But they're over there! In the square!'

'Yes,' said Dr Metaxas again.

'They're just like silly children,' said Aphrodite indulgently.

'Yes, but –'

'Everyone in Athens carries a gun,' said Dr Metaxas. 'At least, quite a lot of people do.'

And, now that Seymour looked, he saw that it was true. Many of the men wore short loose jackets which concealed their belts. And in the belt, very often, was stuck a revolver. It was like some kind of Wild West town.

'It harks back,' said Dr Metaxas, 'as everything in Athens does, to the days when they lived in the countryside. Everyone had a gun then. You needed it against the brigands. Of course, that was forty years ago. But when they moved into the towns, they brought the guns with them.'

'But doesn't it lead to . . .?'

All you would need in the East End, thought Seymour, on top of everything else, would be guns.

'Mayhem?'

'Sometimes. But not as often as you might think. They fire them, these days, mostly into the air.'

'They've got a law about it,' said Aphrodite casually. 'Against carrying guns, that is. But no one pays much attention.'

The people at the tables had barely looked up.

'It's not that the Greeks are against having laws,' said Dr

Metaxas. 'It's just that they think they apply only to other people.'

A cooling puff of breeze went through the square sending up little ruffles of dust. Dr Metaxas put a hand over his glass. When the ruffle had passed there was a thin film of dust on the table. Not far from where they were sitting was a small garden planted with orange trees. The oranges were covered with dust too.

'Among the things I've been looking at today,' said Seymour, 'is how the poison could have got into the harem.'

'Still on that cat?' said Dr Metaxas.

'Yes. You see, once you're in the harem, you're not allowed out. So you couldn't have gone out and got it. You would have to find some means of bringing it in. And the trouble about that is that no one is allowed into the harem either. The poison would have to have been given to the eunuchs at the door, in the same way as everything else, even food.'

'They might have brought the poison to Athens with them,' objected Dr Metaxas.

'Even if they had acquired it in Salonica, the constraints of the harem would still have applied. And the same is true if they had acquired it in Istanbul. So I have been trying to find a way in which poison could have entered the harem.'

'And have you found it?'

'It could have come in in the guise of medicine. The ladies of the harem are presumably allowed to ask for medicine. They might even have got a doctor to provide it. And there have been plenty of opportunities recently, with all the doctors who have been called in for the Sultan, for them to see a doctor.'

'Yes?'

'You, yourself, for instance, have been called in.'

'True, but I did not prescribe poison.'

'No, of course not. But what you prescribed might have been switched. Poison for medicine.'

'Well, I suppose it might,' said Dr Metaxas. 'But –'

'Could you tell me about what happened when you were called in? The procedure?'

'It was barbaric. Ridiculous! I wasn't even allowed to see her. She stood behind a curtain all the time!'

Aphrodite laughed.

'No, it's true!' Dr Metaxas insisted. 'I wasn't allowed to examine her. All I could go on was her description of her symptoms.'

'And could you proceed on that basis?'

'I did proceed. A physician, as I'm sure you've spotted, is a man with principles. And one of the principles is never to refuse a good fat fee.'

'Did you, in fact, prescribe something?'

'I did. For constipation. I assumed that her problems were largely the same as those of the cat. In fact, I detected considerable similarities with the cat.'

'It's monstrous,' said Aphrodite. 'Keeping women like that!'

'The results are much the same,' said Dr Metaxas. 'Neuroticism, obesity –'

'You wrote out a prescription, presumably?'

'I did.'

'And then what? Did you give it to her? Personally?'

'I didn't get close enough to give her anything. As I say, she remained behind the curtain all the time. I handed the prescription to one of the eunuchs.'

He smiled ironically.

'So,' he said, 'is that what you wanted? An explanation of how it got into the harem? Something at least for you to investigate. If you have nothing better to do.'

He made a dismissive gesture.

70

'Pah!' he said. 'Eunuchs, harem, poison – and this in Athens! An enclave of Ottoman backwardness in a city of cars and flying machines! Cat!' he said scornfully. 'You are wasting your time, Mr Seymour.'

Seymour felt inclined to agree with him.

Chapter Five

Seymour had a deep scepticism for government, and that scepticism grew as he walked up the drive to the Sultan's residence the next morning. The increase in guards promised at the meeting he had attended looked as if it had been implemented. The Greek guards had grown in numbers and now spread right across the road, which was obstructed by a hastily erected road block. Further up the drive the Ottoman soldiers, bayonets pointing, were out in force. At the gates to the house French military uniforms mingled with English naval uniforms and there was an unusually businesslike air.

Inside the house there were cavasses everywhere. Seymour captured one and asked if he could speak to Orhan Eser, the Acting-Vizier's assistant. A cavass went off but did not return. After some time Seymour collared another cavass, but with the same result. In the end he went to the kitchen, which was about the only place where there seemed to be people, and people he could talk to without going through intermediaries.

In the kitchen everyone was scurrying around except for the small girl, Chloe, who was standing by the door anxiously chewing her fingers. Someone put a huge tray of dishes into her arms and she rushed off. Other servants came in and collected trays. Breakfast, it appeared, was being served late this morning.

One of the servants stopped for a moment near Seymour and he took the chance to ask what was going on.

'Haven't you heard? The Sultan's been poisoned!'

Poisoned! He seized one of the cavasses and demanded to be taken to the Sultan's apartments.

Outside the large, ornate doors a crowd of people were waiting: picturesquely dressed guards, dark-suited officials and a group of elderly men whom Seymour guessed to be doctors. Among them was Dr Metaxas. He caught Seymour's eye and came across.

'Again!' he said, and shrugged his shoulders.

'Again?'

'We've been here before.'

'He's not . . . dying, then?'

'Unfortunately not,' said Dr Metaxas.

Someone called him and he went back to the doctors. A little later they went through the large doors.

Seymour saw Orhan Eser.

'Can I be of use?'

Orhan Eser considered.

'Possibly,' he said. 'Wait here.'

He disappeared.

'It looks as if it's real this time,' said someone in the crowd.

'It will be one day,' said another.

Orhan Eser came back.

'You are to see Abd-es-Salaam,' he said. 'Only he can't see you just now. Please wait.'

Seymour waited. After a while the crowd thinned out. The officials went away. The doctors were all inside. Eventually only the guards were left.

There was little he could do here. He went back to the kitchen.

The little girl was still standing by the door, still chewing her fingers.

'Hello!' he said. 'Are you Chloe?'

She gave him a frightened look.

'Yes, sir,' she said, almost inaudibly. She was so young that she wasn't wearing a veil. Or perhaps she wasn't a Muslim.

'You've been taking the food to the harem, have you?'

73

'Yes, sir.'

'Perhaps I'll come with you the next time you go. I want to speak to the eunuchs.'

'They're having their breakfast.'

'Oh. Right.'

She hesitated, and then seemed to pluck up her courage.

'I have to go back to fetch the dishes,' she confided.

'Perhaps I'll come with you then and you can show me where it is.'

'Yes, sir.'

He smiled at her encouragingly.

'You're a local girl, are you?'

'Yes, sir.' And then, after a moment: 'I live up in the mountains. We have a farm there.'

'Oh, yes.' Then a thought struck him. 'You're not anything to do with Ari, the milkman, are you?'

'His niece.'

'And you've come to work here?'

'Had to. There's nothing up in the mountains.'

'Do you like it here?'

She thought.

'It's very big.'

'And are they nice to you?'

'Amina beats me sometimes.'

'She's hard on you, is she?'

'She's an old devil!' she said, with sudden energy.

'What about the eunuchs?'

'They're all right. Usually. They don't pay much attention to me.' Then, after a moment, confidingly: 'They're a bit odd.'

'And what about the ladies of the harem?'

'I don't see much of them. I usually stop at the door. But the Lady Irina was nice to me.'

'Oh? When was that?'

'There was a dish. And it was chipped. And the eunuch said I'd done it, though I hadn't. And he hit me. And the Lady Irina said, "Do that again and I'll hit you!" The way she spoke! You wouldn't speak to a man like that up in our

74

village, I can tell you! I was frightened they might hurt her. Amina told me afterwards that the eunuchs had complained to Abd-es-Salaam but that Abd-es-Salaam had said, "Count yourselves fortunate that she didn't have you for breakfast!" And she patted my hand and told me not to cry and that if they were ever nasty to me again I was to come to her.'

'Well, that was very kind of her. Although I don't know how you could go to her, because you can't go in the harem, can you?'

'I don't usually go in. But sometimes they invite me in and the eunuchs don't mind, they let me slip past. And they show me their dresses. They have such lovely dresses. And sometimes the Lady Samira lets me put on her shoes. But I prefer the Lady Irina. She gives me chocolates.'

Another cat, thought Seymour, for them to play with.

When Chloe went to collect the dirty dishes from the harem, Seymour went with her. The eunuch on duty at the door raised his eyebrows.

'I am afraid, sir, that you cannot –'

'I am not seeking entrance,' said Seymour swiftly. 'It is you I have come to see.'

'Me?'

This was clearly troubling and the eunuch looked anxiously over his shoulder.

'I have some small questions I want to put.'

'I am afraid, sir, that I could not – not without permission, that is.'

'And of course I could get it. But I do not wish to bother Abd-es-Salaam just now when he has so much on his mind. And they are just small questions, hardly worth making a fuss over.'

'Well . . .'

'Of course, I could if necessary. And will.'

There was something to be said, he had decided, for

Lady Samira's high-handed approach, especially when dealing with Ottoman bureaucracy.

'If you insist.'

'Well . . .' said the eunuch, looking over his shoulder again desperately. But reinforcement did not appear. Reinforcement, probably, was keeping sensibly out of sight.

'Good. Then I will put my questions. They are, as I said, just small ones.'

Small or large, they were not, the eunuch clearly felt, for him to answer. Best to fall back at once on traditional defence: the blank wall. No one and nothing was allowed to pass into or out of the harem. Food? Well, of course. But nothing else. Medicine? Well, possibly. But only with Abd-es-Salaam's permission, of course, the eunuch added hastily. So whoever was on duty would always seek permission before admitting any medicine? Naturally. And when had this last occurred? Well . . . The eunuch didn't think it *had* occurred. Not recently.

Seymour said that that was funny because he had gathered that several of the royal ladies had recently taken advantage of the doctors' visits to the Sultan to consult them on their own behalf.

The eunuch did not think so.

That, too, was strange, Seymour said, because he had spoken to the doctors and that was what they had said.

Well, perhaps there had been an isolated case or two.

Could the eunuch supply the names and the occasions?

Alas, the eunuch couldn't. There was so much coming and going.

But he had just said that there wasn't. That no one or nothing could get in?

The Effendi must have misunderstood him.

And the medicine? Medicine had been prescribed. Had it been let in? With or without permission? If with, Seymour would be able to confirm that by recourse to Abd-es-Salaam's office. If without . . .

The eunuch blank-walled desperately. But the blank wall

76

did not come down. Seymour was tempted to unleash the Lady Irina on him.

But then the Lady Irina was precisely the person he didn't want to involve over this.

In the corridor, as he was coming back from the harem, he ran into Dr Metaxas.

'You have seen the Sultan? How is he?'

'As well as can be expected.'

'What does that mean?'

'It means as well as you would expect given your initial position.'

'I'm sorry?'

Dr Metaxas sighed.

'Take me, for instance. In my opinion the Sultan is suffering from an over-active and self-pitying imagination. I would expect to find him self-pitying away. And that is precisely what I have found. Whereas . . .'

'Whereas?'

'My colleague, Fahkri Bey, has perceived symptoms consistent with mild arsenic poisoning.'

'I see.'

'Yes. The trouble is, Fahkri Bey is, possibly alone among my colleagues, an experienced, competent physician.'

'He could be right, you mean?'

'We shall have to await the results of the tests.'

'But, meanwhile, the Sultan's life is not in danger?'

'That depends on your initial position.'

'Hmm.'

'There is, though, common ground among us. We are all agreed on the need for continual close monitoring of the patient's condition. We are all professionals,' he said, carrying on down the corridor, 'and we want to keep the money coming in,' he said over his shoulder.

'Your view?' asked Abd-es-Salaam, as they sat in his dimly lit room.

'I have not changed my view,' said Seymour, 'that this is merely the consequence of a trivial harem squabble.'

The Acting-Vizier nodded.

'A stupid dispute between silly women. I think I understand you. You see a dead cat and you think: this is silly, I should not be spending time on this. You wonder what you are doing here.'

'More or less, yes.'

'Despite what happened this morning?'

'If anything happened this morning.'

Abd-es-Salaam nodded again.

'I have, I must admit, sometimes been tempted to share your view. I have sometimes wondered if the Sultan's stomach cramps are merely a physical expression of his natural fears and anxieties. I put this to Fahkri Bey, and he said he had sometimes wondered this too. But not this morning. He thinks the pains are real and caused by the ingestion of a noxious substance. The symptoms, he said, are consistent with mild arsenic poisoning.'

'If that proves to be the case then my view will naturally be affected.'

'Of course, if may be partly right. It may well be a harem matter. Only not a trivial one, not the issue of a silly dispute between foolish women, but something far graver.

'You see,' he went on, 'I see it differently from you. I see a man surrounded, an animal at bay. Imagine a man with power, nearly absolute power. And then suddenly it is snatched away. He feels naked, vulnerable. And this is not just imagination. He really is in danger. In his time wielding power he will inevitably have made enemies. Now is their chance to be revenged. My job is to protect him from them.

'But that is just my first job. My second is to protect him from a different kind of enemy. Do you play chess, Mr Seymour? Imagine a king who has become a pawn. He is now a piece that others can play with, fit to their designs. Possibly take. The Balkans are a turbulent world and there

78

are many players and different designs. And many of these designs involve His Highness.

'So I see a man surrounded. I see a man in the middle of a ring of enemies each of whom may wish to kill him. Well, of course, I am not alone in seeing this and there are other people, some with great power, who, for their own reasons, do not wish to see him killed. They try to guard him, and, of course, I try to guard him too.

'The attack from without, I think I and my allies can guard him from. But an attack from within is a different matter.

'And now, perhaps, you can see why a dead cat may be important. It may mean that an enemy has got behind the defences.

'So I do not dismiss the cat as silly: and I hope, Mr Seymour, that you will not do so either. And you may be right –I think you are – that this is a harem matter. But wrong in thinking that this is just a question of a silly dispute between foolish women. They, too, may be pawns in a much bigger game.'

One small, immediate result of Seymour's interview with Abd-es-Salaam was that when he next went to see the eunuchs, the blank wall had been removed. No one could have been more helpful or more cooperative. They agreed at once to supply a list of the occasions on which the royal ladies had sought medical help. They thought they could work out the occasions on which medicines had passed into the harem. They even agreed to attempt to recover such medicines as they could.

'Do it, if you can, without alerting the royal ladies. You might use the maids.'

They thought they might.

'Although, of course,' Seymour said to the Acting-Vizier's assistant afterwards, 'the eunuchs themselves are not above suspicion. It might be better if some way could be found in which I myself could conduct a search.'

In the harem? Orhan Eser was aghast. No, he said, shaking his head firmly, it definitely could not. Not all walls were dismountable.

Seymour thought he was beginning to work Orhan Eser out now. He was a sort of personal secretary to the Acting-Vizier and so in a position of considerable power. He 'had the ear' of Abd-es-Salaam, as the Eastern world put it. It was through him that everyone had to approach the Acting-Vizier and through him that all instructions came outward. He was clearly a person to stay on the right side of.

What Seymour could not work out, though, was what he was doing here. There was no future for an able, presumably ambitious, man at the court of an exiled Sultan. What induced him to stay? Loyalty? Some strong family bond? Or hope for something better, a change in circumstances, perhaps a return to Istanbul or power, where he could hope to benefit?

Or was – and this was the point – his allegiance elsewhere? Ambitious men in Turkey these days were usually on the side of the new reforming Government. Could they have placed him here? To keep an eye on the Sultan? Or be in a position to act, should action, for some reason, become necessary.

In the house he had had the feeling that all the windows were closed. They weren't, of course: it was just that the shutters over the windows were closed. The windows were left open to allow what breeze there was to come through the slots. The effect of the shutters, though, was to make the house dark. In many of the rooms lamps were kept burning all the time, which reinforced the impression he always had when he was there that it was night. It seemed odd to have this impression when you were in bright, sunlit Athens. He wondered if the Greeks had the

80

impression, too. Or did they do the same when they were in their own houses, shut out the sun and retreat into the shade and the cool? He had a feeling that if they did, the retreat would not be as total, that it would smack too much of the old Ottoman practices that they were so anxious to reject. He did feel, every time he entered the Sultan's house, that he was entering a different world, slipping back in time: the Greeks would certainly see it like that.

It was a relief, at the end of the morning, to come out into the sunshine. But by this time the heat had built up and as he walked down the drive he could hear the pine cones cracking open in the pine woods in which the house was set. The trees provided some relief from the sun and it was only when he stepped out of the drive that he experienced the full blast of the heat. In a moment his shirt was wringing wet and sweat was pouring down his face. He was wearing a suit and a collar and tie – a royal residence demanded it – and envied the people in their casual open shirts and easy trousers.

Not that he saw many people as he walked back to his hotel. In the square people had deserted the tables and retreated inside. The carriages were seeking out shade for their drivers' siestas. Shops were closing. In the back streets stallholders were creeping under their stalls. The smell of ripe fruit hung everywhere.

At the hotel he found a message from Dr Metaxas, inviting him to dinner. Aphrodite would call for him – in case he had forgotten the way – and take him to the house. After collecting her father, he wondered?

But no, when he came down, she was standing there alone. Seymour was pleased. This was one of the perks of working abroad. Back in the East End there were no pretty girls at the end of the day. There were girls waiting, of course, and some of them were pretty, but they weren't that sort.

The East End generally was a conservative place, at least as far as attitudes to women went. The immigrants had brought stricter habits with them from their native countries and guarded their daughters jealously. Old Tsakatellis had warned him about this, too. In Greece, he said, they're not like they are here. Family honour is concerned, so watch your step! And certainly Tsakatellis guarded his own family honour carefully. Seymour hadn't seen Angelica Tsakatellis since they had been in primary school together. How was it she had never married? Maybe he should look her up.

Or maybe he shouldn't. That was the thing about family honour. Anyway, Tsakatellis was probably out of date. He certainly was, if the Metaxases were anything to go by. Sending your daughter to fetch a strange man? You wouldn't do that in the East End!

Aphrodite seemed to have quite a lot of freedom. Maybe it went with her being at university. Seymour had never met a woman who was at university before. It was like coming across a Blériot machine.

There was talk of the Blériot machines at the Metaxases' that evening. This was because their son, Andreas, was there and he didn't seem to be able to talk about much else. He was a nice lad, fair, like his mother, and with a new moustache. The family pride in him was evident: so, at least on Dr Metaxas's part, was misgiving.

It came out when Seymour asked him about the university. About his studies, Andreas was vague; about his friends, enthusiastic. But his enthusiasm centred mainly on what he did outside university, and that was largely to do with flying. It had been given a great boost by the arrival of Stevens and they were now spending almost every afternoon at his workshop.

'I sent you to university,' Dr Metaxas growled. 'Not to an army workshop.'

'It's one of the best workshops in the world,' Andreas said earnestly. 'For flying machines, that is.'

'Stevens says so, does he?'

'And he knows. He's trained in France. He's been with Blériot ever since he read in the newspaper that he was going to attempt to fly the Channel. He says he knew at once that this was going to alter the world. And he wanted to be part of it. And I want to be part of it, too,' said Andreas, his face shining.

'Yes, well, just be part of the university for a few months longer, will you?' said Dr Metaxas.

'Andreas, you know this is too expensive for you,'said Mrs Metaxas. 'It's all right for George. His father can afford it. We cannot.'

'But that's the point!' cried Andreas. 'That's the whole point. Of course I can't afford it. But I won't have to, when the Government gets the new machines.'

'You think they'll be like your friend, George, and let you have a go whenever you want to?' said Dr Metaxas sarcastically.

'They'll need pilots.'

'Now, just a minute –'

'They'll need pilots. Especially when the war comes.'

'Andreas, you're not thinking –'

'Mother, it's my big chance. They'll need pilots. Only three of them to start with, that's true, but I've got a good chance. I'm one of the best flyers, Stevens says that. And Stevens is bound to have a big say in who is chosen. He says he'll put in a word for me –'

'Andreas, you're not to do this!'

'Mother, it gives me my chance. If I don't do this, I'll never get a chance to fly properly. To be a professional pilot.'

'Professional –' began Dr Metaxas.

'But, Andreas,' said Mrs Metaxas, 'they'll only want you if there's a war.'

'Well, I know, but – look, Mother, it's not as if I'm going to be hurt. That's the thing about the machine. You're up there out of the way. It's not like being on the ground fighting. Now that really would be dangerous. But all

I would be doing is looking. Just looking, Mother, and then going back and telling them what I had seen.'

'One thing is clear to me,' said Dr Metaxas, 'and that is that intelligence is not a requirement in a pilot!'

'I think it's very exciting!' declared Aphrodite.

'My family has known fighting,' said Mrs Metaxas. 'It has known killing. And I am not having my son killed in this foolish way.'

'Mother, if there's a war . . . Look, I'll have to fight anyway. And this is a much safer way of fighting.'

'You are not fighting.'

'Mother, if everyone else –'

'You are not fighting. Hear me!'

'Hear your mother!' echoed Dr Metaxas.

They sat in awkward silence for a moment and then Aphrodite rose and fetched coffee. Free spirit she might be, but in the house she was a dutiful daughter. And Andreas, kick against the pricks as he might, also seemed to be a dutiful son. The family seemed to be a very close one, and Seymour could relate to that as it was very like the way it was in his own family. Very close but also oppressive. He remembered how it had been when he had decided to go into the police.

This being the East End, the police were the enemy. Quite a lot of the people there had fallen foul of the authorities in their own country and when they had come to England their first instinct, reinforced, it must be said, by the treatment they got, was to distrust the police. Seymour's family had been no exception. His Polish grandfather had left Poland in a hurry just ahead of the Czar's police. In England he had confined his revolutionary activities largely to his speech but his heart, as he regularly declared, pounding it, was against the Government. Seymour's mother, who had seen her father die in a Hapsburg jail, was more muted but probably more intransigent. His sister, a teacher in a tough East End

84

school, and a member of most of the loony revolutionary societies that Seymour spent his time trying to close down, took after her. His father, a rebel in his own way, would have nothing to do with any of it, police or politics. Steer clear of the lot, was his frequently expressed advice.

So when Seymour announced his decision to go into the police, the whole family, for different reasons, was against him.

'No one will speak to you,' his mother declared. In fact, they all spoke to him. Sorrowfully, it is true. However, as Old Tsakatellis said, if you grow up with someone, the bonds between you are stronger than the bonds between you and the Government.

His sister was the worst. 'Traitor!' she said. But then, she had been abusing him ever since he was born, so he didn't mind that too much.

In the closed world of the East End, it was a decisive step. 'So,' said Seymour, 'what would you prefer, me breathing down your neck or the Old Street Gang? At least I don't carve you up.' Carving up? On that, his mother had taken a line very similar to that of Mrs Metaxas. 'Listen, don't you go near –!' And on the first occasion that he had, his grandfather, thinking he might need assistance, had taken out his old sabre from behind the wardrobe and come down the street to lend a hand.

So he felt he knew how it was for young Andreas. Indeed, he had some sympathy for him. Over the desire to fly, that was, not over the going to war. But wasn't there a bit of the comic opera about all this going-to-war stuff? You didn't go to war like this, did you?

One thing that came out of the evening was an invitation from Andreas to visit the famous workshop, and the next morning Seymour went over there. One of the Blériot machines was standing in the forecourt. It had two wings, one above the other, and two cockpits, one behind, so that it could carry a passenger: an observer, as Stevens put it.

85

Stevens, in the middle of a group of young men, was explaining how the ailerons worked. A new mechanism had been fitted which was, he said, twice as effective as the old. He was a good explainer and knew his stuff. The group listened intently. There were two mechanics there, who were interested in the technical side, but the rest of the group were young Andreases, interested in flying the machines not mending them. Stevens knew this and pitched his talk accordingly, explaining what the new ailerons would enable them to do in the air.

'You won't really know until you've tried them out,' he said. 'But when you do, you'll be surprised. Don't be too heavy the first time or two that you try them.'

Andreas asked if he could try out the controls and see how it felt. He climbed up into the cockpit and worked the ailerons for a while.

Seymour, standing so close and seeing a flying machine close up for the first time, was struck by how fragile it seemed to be. When he touched a wing, the whole machine tipped towards him. They were, in the end, he thought, only a kite with a motor-bicycle engine attached.

He said this to Stevens and Stevens laughed and said that was exactly what they were, but that was where the fun lay. You were so close to the air and the wind and the sky. It was, he said, like sailing but with nothing there but the sail. You quivered, he said, with the aircraft, at the slightest touch of the air. The engine would drive you through but all the time you had to be responding to what the air currents were doing.

'There's nothing like it,' he said. 'You don't really know until you've been up.'

He asked Andreas if he would like to take the machine out. Andreas flushed with pleasure and said he would. Someone brought him helmet, goggles and gloves and he put them on.

Stevens leaned over the side of the cockpit.

'Remember!' he said. 'Not too heavy, the first time or two. Until you've got used to them.'

He stepped away, and a moment later, the Blériot machine taxied out on to the runway. They watched it take off.

'You don't go with him, then?' said Seymour.

'These boys are experienced pilots. At least, some of them are. Andreas certainly is. He'd be all right.'

They walked back to the workshop together. For some reason, probably because they'd met at the Embassy, Stevens assumed him to be one of the Embassy staff.

'You know,' he said, 'I'm surprised that you haven't got anyone out.'

'Anyone out?'

'You know, on the military side. A military attaché, or someone like that. Someone knowledgeable who could report. Because this war is going to be different, with the flying machines, and our people ought to be following it.'

'I expect word will get back.'

'They ought to have someone out,' Stevens insisted. 'There's a lot to learn. About tactics, strategy, how best to use them, that sort of stuff. And supplies. The supply problem will be different.'

'Yes, I'm sure,' said Seymour, wondering if this was the moment when he could slip away.

'Because there isn't much time.'

'Time?'

'Before the next war starts. The big one.'

What a load of bollocks, thought Seymour.

Then.

Afterwards, Seymour returned to the Sultan's residence. All was quiet there now. The Sultan, Orhan Eser said, was resting.

'How is he?'

Orhan Eser hesitated.

'He seems better. He has, of course, a strong constitution and seems to have shaken off the effects of the poison, although his stomach is still rather disturbed.'

'It was poison, was it?'

'Fahkri Bey is confident, although we await the result of the tests.'

'That does rather alter things.'

'I don't know that it does,' said Orhan Eser. 'We have had our suspicions for some time and now it appears that they have been confirmed.'

'I mean, from my point of view. Ought I not to be working on the Sultan and not on the cat?'

'The two are connected. Continue with the cat for the time being.'

They were standing by an open door which led out on to a small balcony. In the distance there was a now familiar sound. The Blériot machine approached and swooped low over the house.

Orhan Eser went quickly outside.

'They are doing this all the time,' he said. 'It must be deliberate. Is it a threat? Or a warning?'

'I think they may be just playing around.'

'Does one play,' asked Orhan Eser, 'with machines as dangerous and expensive as this?'

'I think they may be trying out a new fitting.'

He told Orhan Eser about the ailerons and about his visit that morning.

'They're just young men. Rich amateurs playing with their toys.'

'The Government has ordered them more machines. And they won't be flown by amateurs.'

Chapter Six

Aphrodite, sitting beside him in a small restaurant in the Plaka, was questioning him about the Sultan's harem. How did those poor women manage to exist? How could they bear to go on living like that? It really brought it home, she said, how it must have been in the old days, seventy years before, when Greece was still part of the Ottoman Empire and the Ottomans ruled in Athens. Suppose she had been alive then: how would she have fared? Might she herself have been in a harem somewhere? Her father would have fought against it, she was sure. But would he have had any choice? Suppose some powerful Ottoman had come along and said, 'I'll have her.' What could he or she have done about it? She would have finished up in a harem just like those poor creatures Seymour had been telling her about. Phew, there was a thought!

They had just come down from the Acropolis. The previous evening, at the Metaxases', Seymour had mentioned his desire to see something of the city while he was here. Back in London, when Old Tsakatellis had suggested this, Seymour had thought he might be too busy. 'Too busy,' Tsakatellis had said incredulously, 'to see the Parthenon?' On reflection Seymour had thought that would be, indeed, to put too narrow a construction on his duties. The Metaxases had supported him. The Acropolis, the Parthenon – why not? And why not at sunset? And why not with Aphrodite to show him round? Why not, indeed, thought Seymour.

He was warming to Aphrodite. When he had first encountered her, looming over the table, dressed all in black, arms folded, commanding her father, she had put the fear of God into him. On further acquaintance, though, it became clear that there were other sides to her: that business, for example, of wanting to be a Blériot mechanic! And training to be a doctor! Even going to university. Back in England no one went to university except people like the Secretaries at the Embassy. Certainly no one in the East End went to university. And no woman had a hope of becoming a doctor.

Seymour, who had occasionally daydreamed of going to university himself, was sufficiently well read in the newspapers to suspect that he was meeting a specimen of 'the New Woman'. The newspapers and journals back in London were full of her. Down in Whitechapel, however, New Women were few on the ground. Except, possibly, his sister, who didn't count. How odd that he should have to come to Greece to find one! (This was one of the treasures of Greece that Tsakatellis had not mentioned.) Having come across her, though, Seymour was disposed to pursue the acquaintance further. And what better place for sci-entific enquiry than the Parthenon at sunset?

Aphrodite, too, a genuine scientist, after all, felt that she should not let slip this opportunity of studying a male of a different species than those she was accustomed to, particularly one who came from so exotic a place as . . . Whitechapel, was it? She knew little about London's East End but took it for granted that the chapel *was* white, like the Parthenon, perhaps, only, obviously, since that was Greek, less beautiful. Anyway, the subject was worth pur-suing, especially at the Parthenon at sunset, and an hour or so later they descended the hill having established a close, if not entirely scientific, rapport.

The restaurant was complete with candles and vine leaves and on each table was a little Greek flag: a new fashion, said Aphrodite and one which always put her father in a rage.

'He must be often in a rage these days,' said Seymour, for all along the street there were flags, hanging from windows, draped from balconies and suspended from the street lamps.

'Oh, that's because of the soldiers,' said Aphrodite. 'They're leaving tomorrow.'

'Leaving?'

'For Salonica. They say. My father says not. He says they'll stop when they get two miles out of town and all the crowds have turned back. They'll sit on the ground in the shade and have a drink. There is, he says, a saving spirit of realism in Greeks which usually, but always at the eleventh hour, stops them from doing anything too stupid.'

Later in the evening a baggy-trousered musician came in from the street and began playing a pipe. On closer inspection Seymour saw that the pipe was made from the barrel of a gun.

'A sign of the times?' he suggested.

Aphrodite frowned.

'A sign of the eternal Greek ability to put things to better use,' she said.

But Seymour wondered if it was also a sign of the eternal Balkan ability to find a pretext for fighting one's neighbours. At the Parthenon Aphrodite had shown him the still evident damage caused by the great explosion of 1687 when a stray shell from the besieging Venetian forces had ignited the power magazine that the Ottomans, who happened to be occupying the Parthenon at that time, had casually stored within its columns.

The next morning Seymour thought he had better go to the Embassy and check.

'Oh, yes,' said the First Secretary, 'they're definitely moving out. But probably not very far. There's an element of posturing in Greek politics. It comes from them being a democracy. They have to work up popular feeling before they can do anything. Usually the feeling subsides before they get to doing it.'

'So there isn't going to be a war?'

'Oh, I wouldn't say that. It's just that there may be a prolonged period of sparring first. And that, of course, is where you come in.'

'Me?'

'The cat business. The manoeuvring around the Sultan.'

'You think that won't come to anything?'

'Oh, it might. But the longer it goes on without coming to anything, the better, from our point of view. The greater the chance of peace. They need a pretext, you see, for going to war. It looks bad to go to war without an excuse.'

'I'm sorry. I still don't see where I come in.'

'Well, look, old chap, the cat is hardly important, is it? So the more time everybody spends on it, the better. It sort of deflects their energies from more dangerous things.'

'So you don't really want me to find out –'

'Oh, we do, old boy, we do. Only not too quickly.'

Despite that, Seymour returned to the Sultan's residence, where he was now on familiar terms with the soldiers guarding, the kitchen staff, and Orhan Eser.

'How is the Sultan this morning?'

'He has, I am afraid, a severe attack of stomach cramps.'

'Ah, well, this must be a relief to you.'

'Relief?'

'After your fears. That it might be something worse.'

'It does not end the fears. For what gave rise to the stomach cramps? That must be looked into.'

'Well, yes, I see.'

Fortunately, he, Seymour, wasn't going to be doing the looking.

He asked if he could speak to the maid, Zenobia.

*　　*　　*

'You are Zenobia?'

'That is true.'

'And you serve in the harem?'

'That also is true.'

'And whom do you serve particularly?'

'The Lady Fatima.'

'I want you to cast your mind back to the day when the cat was poisoned. Do you remember that day?'

'Oh, yes, Effendi. Who would not!'

'Could you tell me where you were when the cat was feeding?'

'I was with the Lady Fatima, helping her to dress.'

'And at some point, I understand, you saw the cat. Is that right?'

'Yes, Effendi.'

'And where was it?'

'I saw it twice, Effendi. The second time it was dead.'

'And that was in the room where Miriam had put the bowl?'

'Yes, Effendi.'

'But that was not where you saw the cat the other time?'

'No, Effendi.'

'Where was that?'

'In the room next door.'

'And what was the cat doing?'

'It was sitting on the Lady Irina's lap.'

'And what was the Lady Irina doing?'

'She was feeding it chocolates.'

'Did you see the chocolates?'

'See the chocolates?'

'Was she taking them from a box?'

'Yes, Effendi. On the table beside her.'

'Could you find the box for me?'

'I am sorry, Effendi. I do not think so. The box is no longer there.'

'Where do you think it could be?'

'I do not know, Effendi. Perhaps all the chocolates have been eaten.'

'You are sure the box is no longer there?'

'Yes, Effendi. Because later that day I went to find it. I thought I would like a chocolate myself, and those were very good chocolates, better than the ones the Lady Fatima has.'

'And the box was no longer there?'

'No, Effendi.'

'Perhaps the Lady Irina had it?'

'It may be so, Effendi.'

'Was she doing anything else when she was with the cat? Apart from feeding it chocolates?'

'No, Effendi.' She hesitated. 'At least . . .'

'Yes?'

'She was talking.'

'Ah! Who to?'

'The cat, Effendi.'

'And what was she saying?'

'"Eat that, you filthy brute! Go on, stuff yourself!"'

'That was what she said?'

'Yes, Effendi, I remember it well, for I said to myself, "That is no way to speak to the Sultan's cat!" But so it was.'

'And then?'

'The Lady Fatima called, and I went back to her. And the next time I saw the cat, it was dead.'

'Would you like a chocolate?' asked the Lady Irina: and burst into laughter. 'You are going to ask me about the chocolates, aren't you? I guessed as much as soon as I heard that you had been talking to that little bitch, Zenobia.'

'Well, all right, then: what about the chocolates?'

'I wanted to stuff the brute until it would be sick. All over him!'

'His Highness?'

'Naturally. I wanted him to come in and find me sitting with the brute on my lap. As I told you. His Highness loves that sort of thing. Beauty and the Beast. No, not that. Beauty and Beauty, rather. He really thinks that nasty cat is beautiful. He likes to see us together. A touch of the domestic, I think he thinks. As if a Sultan could ever know anything about the domestic! When I came into the harem I expected to have to live out his fantasies. But I thought they would be nude on a tiger-skin, that sort of thing. Not nursing a bloody cat! When all the poor man was wanting was someone to be kind to him on a cold winter's evening.'

'Let's get back to the chocolates.'

'Well, as I say, I was sitting there with the nasty brute on my lap. I knew he'd love it when he came in and saw us. I would hand the brute to him, saying, "Now, my dear, go to your master," holding him carefully so that he wouldn't be sick until he got there. And then it would all come out, and he would have to go away and change, and wouldn't bother me again for the rest of the day.'

'You really expect me to believe all that?'

'Certainly!'

'You weren't feeding the cat the chocolates for some other purpose?'

'Other purpose? You don't think I would be feeding him them because he liked them, do you?'

'No, I wouldn't go as far as that. I was just wondering if the chocolates were still as they had been when they came to you.'

'Still –? Oh, I see what you mean. You mean, had I put poison in them? Well, it wouldn't have been worth it, would it? If, as I suspect, you suppose I had poisoned the milk already.'

'Did the chocolates have marzipan in them?'

'*Marzipan*!?'

'Perhaps to disguise the taste. Of the milk.'

'Well, I'd never thought of that. Marzipan? No, I don't

think so. As I recalled, they had cherry liqueur, and brandy, and –'

'Have you any of the chocolates left?'

'Alas, no. That filthy brute devoured them all. Or almost all, I believe. I gave some to His Highness as well. Why, would you like some? I expect I can find –'

'No, thank you. Lady Irina, this is a fine story but it is not quite the same as the story you told me originally. When I first talked to you, you told me that you had gone into the room, the room where the milk was, to pick up the cat so that you could have it on your lap when the Sultan came.'

'That's right. And I did pick it up, and that's when I started giving it the chocolates.'

'No.'

'No?'

'You told me the first time that you *didn't* pick it up, that it was already starting to be sick, and that you left it and went back to your own room.'

'Did I say that? Well, good heavens! I must have remembered it wrongly. But which account was wrong? Look, it doesn't matter much, though, does it: one of them must have been right.'

'Or both wrong.'

'Perhaps I had better try and remember again?'

'Don't bother. Or, rather, yes, do bother. But start from a different point. Let me help you. You went into the room, as you told me the first time. But the cat wasn't being sick. It had, in fact, rejected the milk, perhaps because of its smell or taste. You picked it up and took it into the other room, where you started feeding it chocolates. Possibly with marzipan in, which would disguise the smell and taste, and then you put it back into the first room, where it drank the milk. And then it was sick.'

'Well, I'm blessed! So the chocolates weren't poisoned? And the milk was? So it wasn't me who did it, after all! It was someone else, Talal, for instance, who had put the poison in the milk –'

'My Lady!' protested Talal. 'I was having breakfast!'

'Conveniently. Along with your accomplices.'

'No, no, no –'

'I have an idea,' Irina said to Seymour, 'which may help you. What you need to do is find someone who saw me pick up the cat the first time and take it into the other room, and then saw me put it back before it started on the milk. Not someone who saw me giving it chocolates, there's no dispute about that. And I think I know someone you might talk to. Try Zenobia. Who has such a close, very close, relationship with the Lady Samira. And such an unblemished reputation for honesty. Hasn't she, Talal?'

'Well . . .'

'Hasn't she?'

As the morning wore on, Seymour became increasingly conscious of the activity of the Blériot machines. Even inside the house you could hear them. They swooped repeatedly low over the house; or perhaps they were circling over the city and just happened to be turning at that point. Several times Orhan Eser went out to look and once Seymour went with him.

All three Blériot machines were in the air together. When they banked over the house they were so low that he could see the pilots clearly. The Greek soldiers on guard at the end of the drive would give a cheer. The Ottoman soldiers further up regarded them expressionlessly. Orhan Eser shook his head and went back indoors.

The British sailors outside the house, who were as little used as Seymour to seeing flying machines, studied them curiously.

'What keeps them up, then?' one of them asked.

'The wind?'

'It wouldn't be the wind, mate. Otherwise sailing boats would fly.'

'They've got an engine.'

'Maybe it's the speed?'

'Wouldn't like to be up there myself. Suppose there was a storm?'

'You'd have to make back for port a bit sharpish.'

As Seymour went back into the house he saw a movement at one of the upstairs windows. The window, and the others in that part of the house, had been removed and replaced by wooden lattice-work, which meant, he supposed, that it was a harem window. In Istanbul he had been used to seeing them. They gave light and air to the rooms inside. The air was as important as the light, especially if you never went outside. The lattice-work screened the women from being seen; but occasionally you made out a movement behind it. Someone inside was watching the Blériot machines, too.

Late in the morning, towards noon, the machines flew away. You could still see them, however, only now they were circling over a different place some way out of town.

'That'll be where them soldiers are,' said one of the sailors.

'Stopped for lunch?'

'They stopped for lunch about breakfast time, mate. I don't reckon they're aiming to go far.'

'What are the machines doing, then?'

'Trying to cheer them up, I expect. Put a bit of spirit in them.'

'As long as it stops like that,' said Farquhar, the Second Secretary at the Embassy, who had just joined them. He had come to the house earlier in the morning, to enquire after the Sultan's health, Seymour imagined. He asked if Seymour felt like a spot of lunch, and they walked up the drive together and found a small café where they could sit outside.

'We've spoken to Stevens,' Farquhar said.

'Oh, yes?'

'About not letting himself get too involved. We wouldn't want it to look as if Britain was backing one side.'

'Well, no. I can see that. But he's not involved yet, is he?

The new machines they've ordered haven't arrived, surely?'

'Not yet, no. But there's a question about the three privately owned Blériots and how far the army intends to make use of them. They seem to be moving towards commandeering them.'

'Have they the pilots?'

'They're thinking of using volunteers.'

'The ones who normally fly them.'

'That's right. And from what we can make out, Stevens is encouraging it.'

'He's too much of an enthusiast, that's his trouble.'

'Well, we could do with less of his enthusiasm. The thing is, you see, he's on contract, so there's not much we can do about it. The saving grace is that the new machines have not yet arrived and it's going to be some time before they do. By that time it could all be over, one way or another. We thought we were okay, but now he's bringing in these private machines, calling them auxiliaries. So that blurs it. He could claim he's just offering his services to private individuals and if they offer *their* services to the Greek Government, that's nothing to do with him.'

Later in the afternoon the Blériot machines disappeared; refuelling, Seymour imagined. For towards teatime he saw two of them again, this time close to the mountains which lay between Athens and Salonica.

At the time he was taking Aphrodite to the Sultan's residence to have tea with the Sultan's ladies. The evening before she had asked if it might be possible to meet them. Seymour had doubted it but that morning he had put her request to Orhan Eser. The Acting-Vizier's assistant had been taken aback; such a request had not been made before. On reflection he could see no reason why not. It was acceptable for the ladies to have female visitation. Indeed, in Istanbul it had not been uncommon. It hadn't happened since they had left because, well . . . Because Ottomans were Ottomans and Greeks were Greeks, he supposed.

Seymour had pointed out that Aphrodite was the daughter of Dr Metaxas, who had attended on the Sultan, which should surely guarantee her acceptability. He had added that she was a student at the university and hoped to become a doctor herself.

'Really?' said Orhan Eser, astonished; and then he had added something that had surprised Seymour. 'It is right,' he said, 'that there should be women in such professions.' Seymour hadn't seen much evidence of many people sharing that view when he had been in Istanbul, but perhaps things had changed since the 'Young Turks' had come to power. That made him think again, though, about Orhan Eser himself and exactly where his allegiance lay.

The assistant said that he would have to put it to Abd-es-Salaam. 'You can tell him,' said Seymour, 'that it is possible that a woman can learn things in the harem that a man couldn't.' Orhan Eser had looked at him sharply and then nodded. The point, perhaps, had weighed with Abd-es-Salaam for Orhan Eser had returned saying that it was quite acceptable to the Acting-Vizier.

Seymour had wondered whether he should draw on his credit with the Lady Samira and ask for an invitation, but Orhan Eser said it was unnecessary. The ladies would be only too glad of a diversion. However, for form's sake he would ask a eunuch to approach them. In less than no time he received an answer: The royal ladies would be delighted to receive a lady visitor for 'English tea'. Seymour thought he saw Samira's hand in this and guessed that some of his credit had rubbed off on the invitation after all.

He delivered Aphrodite, herself veiled in the name of decency, to Orhan Eser, who passed her to a eunuch, who took her into the harem.

When she came out, Seymour asked her how the tea had gone.

It had all been very strange, said Aphrodite, but not un-nice. They had all crowded round her, asking questions in a variety of languages, most of which Aphrodite could not speak, and fingering her clothes. Aphrodite had dressed up for the occasion but feared she had let Greece down. She had haltingly offered the explanation that she was a poverty-stricken student.

There had been a little silence.

'Student?'

More explanation, and then a barrage of questions in incomprehensible languages, although one or two had spoken Greek and done some translation for the benefit of the others. Finally, the Lady Samira had borne her off so that they could converse alone. Actually, said Aphrodite, the conversation had been somewhat one-sided: Aphrodite had hardly said a word but Samira had said plenty. She had asked Aphrodite about Athens: about its shops, its theatres, its balls, about where Aphrodite went in her carriage when she took a promenade. Aphrodite said that as a student she didn't go in much for promenades. Samira, after a few questions, lost interest in student life and returned to the shops, concentrating on how they differed from the great shops in Paris, which she knew, alas, only by repute.

Then the Lady Irina had seized her.

'She just walked in,' said Aphrodite, amazed, 'and took me out.'

Irina had not been much interested in the Athens shops but very, very interested in Aphrodite's life as a student. She had asked lots and lots of questions: starting, however, from a position of some ignorance, since she had first had to ask Aphrodite what a student *was*. Aphrodite had said that it was someone who was studying so that they could become a lawyer or a teacher, or, as in her own case, a doctor. Irina had been nonplussed: she had always had the impression that you started as a lawyer or whatever and picked things up as you went along. But this learning business sounded a good idea, and she asked Aphrodite a lot of questions about it.

'She spoke with such *hunger*,' said Aphrodite. 'It was rather sad. She was like a tiger in a cage.'

101

Seymour said he wondered how she had got into the harem in the first place.

'Oh, she's a Vlach,' said Aphrodite.

'Vlach?'

'Or Wallach. Like my mother. They're a people who live north of here. Mostly up in the mountains. They're often fair, and in the past that made them much sought after for harems. That was under the Ottomans, of course. And let me tell you that my mother was *not* one of those seized for the harem.'

'I didn't imagine that for one moment,' said Seymour, laughing.

'No, but it was a constant fear for families up there that their daughters might be. I expect Irina was picked up as a child – or perhaps sold. There used to be people who would travel round looking for young girls like that. You know, with the potential to be beautiful. And their families would sometimes sell them because they were so poor – so I wouldn't be surprised if that was how she got into the Sultan's harem.'

And then, said Aphrodite, the other ladies had come and indignantly prised her away from Irina, and they had all sat down on cushions and had tea with rose petals in it, and eaten some disgusting sweet biscuits and incredibly creamy chocolates and then, with some reluctance, the ladies had let her go.

They were sitting at a table in Constitution Square having a drink when the Blériot machines appeared again. They flew low over the square waggling their wings. The people at the tables cheered.

Again there were only two of them.

'The other one's being repaired,' said Aphrodite. 'It's George's. Andreas was hoping to fly it but Stevens says it won't be ready until tomorrow. Andreas is very fed up.'

'What's wrong with it?'

'Something to do with the cables,' Aphrodite frowned.

'Actually, Stevens is very angry. He says he's sure they have been cut.'

'Cut?'

'Yes. Deliberately, he says.'

'But –'

'I know. How can they have been? But he seems sure of it. He was in a terrific rage. You know, he looks on the machines almost as his children and when anything goes wrong with one of them, he takes it personally.'

'Yes, well, if they have been cut –'

'I know. But I don't see how they could have been. It would have meant someone in the workshop . . . But they all deny it. Andreas says the atmosphere there was terrible this afternoon. Of course my mother was relieved that Andreas couldn't fly. He was going to be taking Stevens up and wanted to impress him.'

'Why was he taking Stevens up?'

'Stevens wanted to take a look at things himself. Over towards the mountains. Or even beyond the mountains. My mother was furious when she heard that. She said that it was involving Andreas in the war, and that Stevens had no business to be doing that. The atmosphere in our house is pretty terrible, too, just at the moment.'

Chapter Seven

The eunuchs had done what Seymour had asked. When he went to the house the next morning they presented him with a list of the occasions on which royal ladies had seen a doctor over the last few weeks and of the medicines which had been prescribed. They had even been able to assemble an astonishing array of the medicines themselves. Apparently, the ladies' enthusiasm for seeing doctors did not extend to taking the medicines they prescribed and most of the bottles had hardly been breached.

One exception, Seymour noticed, was some medicine that had been prescribed for the Lady Irina. The bottle was not to be located. Irina assured everybody that that was because she had consumed the contents and then thrown the bottle away.

The medicine, Seymour saw, had been prescribed by Dr Metaxas and Seymour, assuming that he might be found in his usual place in Constitution Square enjoying a liquid breakfast, went to find him.

'The Lady Irina, you say? Well, it probably was. I can't say I made much distinction between those veiled shapes crouching in a corner. But if you say it was, then you're probably right. The medicine? Oh, I remember that! And the complaint: constipation. Severe constipation, if what she said was correct, but of course, it wasn't. She said she had tried everything but nothing had worked. What she wanted was something . . . *formidable*. I think she said, the French word. Well, I have no patience with these spoiled ladies, whose only problem is a lack of self-discipline. So – *formidable* was what she got.

'Could it have been used for any other purpose? Such as? Poisoning! Look, I am a doctor, not the Vizier's Lord High Executioner. Or Venizelos's, for that matter. You were thinking of the cat? We *know* what the cat died of, and it certainly wasn't the medicine universally prescribed for bad cases of constipation. Might it have been switched? Poison substituted for medicine? Well, it might, I suppose. But why go to the bother? Why not just cut the bloody cat's throat?'

Yes, yes, (wearily), he could have the medicines analysed. If Seymour took them to the place where the autopsy had been performed, they would see to all that.

Seymour, used, in the East End, to spending the day on foot, had elected for the most part to do the same in Athens. Foolishly; by mid-morning the heat had built up and by the time he had reached the mortuary his shirt was wringing wet. It was a relief to go into the cool of the mortuary; which was not the way he usually felt about going into mortuaries.

One of the technicians there remembered him from his previous visit with Dr Metaxas and after that it was plain sailing. Certainly they would analyse the medicines he had brought, although they looked at him curiously: 'They weren't giving this cat medicines, too, were they?'

But then it was out into the heat again, which had increased even while he was inside, and into the dust as well, which, he suddenly realized, had whitened his trousers up to the knees. Sensibly, this morning, people were staying indoors to escape the heat and the tables in the square were nearly empty. Seymour continued on though, making for his hotel and a shower.

At the hotel he found a note waiting for him. It was from Aphrodite and asked him if he would minding seeing Andreas, who would call for him at four.

At the appointed hour Andreas was waiting for him downstairs. It was still early by Greek standards and most of the inhabitants of the hotel were still at their siesta, so it was easy to find a place where they could talk without interruption.

'I do not wish to presume on our acquaintance,' Andreas said, slightly nervously, 'but I would be most grateful for your help. And Stevens would. And George, too. And George's father.'

Seymour guessed, from the way he said it, that George's father was someone you did not refuse assistance to if you lived in Athens.

'It's the Blériot.'

'Ah, yes?'

'Someone's been tampering with it. They've cut the cables. Stevens says it was done deliberately.' Andreas looked at Seymour earnestly. 'That's very serious, you know. It could lead to an accident. Or even – someone being killed. Stevens is very angry about it. George's father is, too. He blames the Turks, and says they're really asking for it if they go in for this sort of thing. Of course, we don't know it was the Turks. But Stevens says it's not the sort of thing someone would do accidentally, they'd have to have intended to do it, if you know what I mean. George's father was all for going to the police but Stevens said hold on a bit – he doesn't think much of the police here, and says that if it's reported to them, he's going to be spending the next couple of weeks filling in forms and sitting in offices. Get someone outside to look at it first, he says. And, well, I thought of you,' finished Andreas, wide-eyed.

'Well, thank you. But I'm not sure I'm really an expert on this sort of thing.'

'Stevens jumped at it when I suggested it. He said he thought you'd got your head screwed on and would be able to tell us if he'd got it right. And what we ought to do.'

'Well, of course, I'd be glad to help, but –'

'I know you're here on something else and probably very busy. But my father says you're wasting your time – I'm sorry, I didn't mean it like that. What he said, actually, was that it was terrible that a good man was having to waste his time, and that it was because Governments had put their heads together, instead of having them knocked together – you know my father.'

'Well, I could come along and take a look at it, I suppose. Although . . .'

As they were leaving the hotel, Andreas stopped and said:

'You won't say anything of this to my parents, will you? I mean, if my mother heard – she makes too much of things and if she heard there was a chance of my being – of something happening to me, well, she'd be out of her mind. It's difficult enough at home just at the moment.'

'You see, I don't want to land up with it getting all political,' Stevens explained. 'I know that's the way out here. Andreas has told me all about his father and the Sultan, and about all the doctors getting involved, and all the Governments, too. I don't want anything like that. I'm just a simple engineer. The way I see it, you just mend the machine and put a guard on it to see it doesn't happen again, and then you get back to flying.

'But, of course, things are never quite so straightforward. Putting a guard on it, say – who's going to pay for that? George's father could certainly stand it, and maybe the others could join in, but . . . Of course, I might be able to get the Government to foot the bill, after all, it's in their interests. I could certainly try that, but I don't want to do it if it can be averted. The less you have to do with Government red tape, the better. The truth is that in the end it will probably have to come to that, because the cost will mount up, and the fathers are bound to jib, so . . . Well, as I say, that's what it will probably come to. But before

I go down that road, I'd like to have someone else's opinion. Have I got it all wrong? Is it just an accident?'

'Look,' said Seymour, 'if this is at all technical, then I'm not –'

Stevens shook his head impatiently.

'It's not the technical side. I can handle that. I'll set out the arguments. Then you can try them out on the technicians. They know what's what, and they'll give you straight answers. No, it's what comes after that. The judgement. That's where you come in. You're used to weighing evidence. I mean, you don't just go in, you have to make up your mind first whether it's likely a crime *has* been committed. That's what I want you to do here.'

There wasn't, actually, much doubt about it. The cables had definitely been cut. The technicians said that nobody had been working on anything nearby and that, anyway, it wasn't the kind of thing that a competent technician would do. Someone must have come in during the night. It wouldn't take long. Snip-snip, was all that was required.

'If you knew what you were doing,' said Seymour. 'And how many people in Athens would know enough about Blériot machines to know that?'

'A good point,' said Stevens, frowning.

That, said Seymour, would be one of the things he would be looking at were he conducting an investigation. Which, unfortunately –

'No, no,' said Stevens. 'I appreciate that.'

'You would do better,' said Seymour, 'to call in the local police.'

Stevens made a face.

'God, he said, 'if you knew the trouble I'd had with the local bureaucrats simply over bringing in parts!'

He thought for a moment.

'The thing is,' he said, 'it could all be about to change. They've ordered three more machines, and when they get here, it'll all be under the army. They'll be responsible for security and all that. I'll leave all that side of things to them. I wouldn't need to get involved.'

He was tempted to leave it, Seymour could see.

'It's just in the interim,' said Stevens. 'Before they get there. You see, what I've been thinking of doing is using the private machines as auxiliaries. The lads are very keen. I wouldn't want them to get involved in any action, that wouldn't be right. And, anyway, the war's not started yet. But what they could do is reconnaissance. And that would show what the Blériots were capable of. It would make the case. If the case were good enough, the Government would possibly want to keep them on. That's what I keep telling the lads. There's room for them. Even after the new machines come. Three are not enough.'

He rubbed his chin.

'So I'd like to keep things going. Keep the machines flying. Make the case. And it wouldn't be difficult. The lads are keen. The technicians, too. I mean, they're just hanging around until the new machines get here. There would be no problem about repairing. Or servicing. So it's only security, and that's only for a week or two, until the new machines arrive and the army takes over. Maybe I could just ask my lads to keep a special eye open? That would take care of it during the day. Then during the night, well, the other lads have volunteered to take care of that. They'd sleep beneath the machines. Take it in turns. That's what they've suggested. Keen as mustard.'

As Seymour was leaving, Stevens caught his arm.

'Would you mind doing something for me? Could you talk to your friends at the Embassy and ask them if they've heard anything about anyone else who's negotiating with the Government? Trying to get into the game? Either trying to sell machines, or do what I'm doing, offering back-up.'

'Rivals?'

'That's right. Otherwise I just don't see . . . You're right, of course. You'd need to know something about it to cut the cables. It's not difficult, but you'd need to know what you were doing. Where to do it, for a start. And that's not something an ordinary person would know, not even an ordinary mechanic. So I wondered if there was another party involved.'

The war did not appear to be advancing. The soldiers were still where they had been, a couple of miles out of town. Nor were they likely to move, said the waiters in the hotel. It was too hot to go to war. Not only that; the build-up in the heat suggested that there would be an electric storm that evening. All the roads would turn to mud and if there was one thing worse than heat for fighting in, it was mud. No, they would get fed up if it rained heavily, particularly if it rained all night, and in the morning they would come home. That was the consensus among the waiters and Seymour thought it likely that intelligence gathered from that source was at least as valid as that gathered from aerial reconnaissance.

The Blériot machines were grounded, anyway, because of the storm. During the afternoon the heat continued to build up, the clouds gathered, and out at sea flashes of lightning began to be detected. The flashes were some way off, however, and the storm approached slowly. As the sky clouded over, however, it became stifling.

Seymour had walked to the Sultan's residence and his shirt was dripping again. He reckoned that by the evening he would be on his fourth shirt of the day.

The Sultan's house, however, was dark and cool. The harem shutters were open and again Seymour thought he saw movement behind the lattice-work. He knew enough about the harem now to be fairly sure that by the time he entered the front door, news of his arrival would have spread throughout the house. He half expected to be summoned by Samira.

He went instead, though, to the kitchen, where they

were just beginning their preparations for the evening meal.

'Effendi?'

'I would like to speak to Chloe.'

'Chloe? You mean Amina?'

'I mean Chloe.'

The little kitchen maid was rooted out and appeared before him, wide-eyed and frightened.

'It's all right, Chloe. I just want to ask you a few questions. Like last time.'

Chloe nodded.

'Because I've been thinking over what you said and there are one or two things that I'd like you to tell me more about.'

She nodded again.

'Now I know you like the Lady Irina.'

'She was kind to me.'

'And stopped the eunuch from beating you.'

'She said that if he beat me, she would beat him!' said Chloe proudly.

'I remember. And I'll bet he's not laid a finger on you since.'

Chloe's worried face dissolved into smiles.

'She is my protector,' she said.

'Do you know what I think?' said Seymour. 'I think she is your friend.'

Chloe beamed.

'And you are hers.'

She nodded vigorously.

'Now you told me that sometimes they let you go into the harem.'

Chloe's worried look returned.

'Sometimes,' she whispered.

'Just occasionally. And didn't you tell me that once the Lady Samira let you try on her shoes? And the Lady Irina gave you chocolates.'

Chloe's face lit up.

'And they talked to you, I expect?'

111

'Oh, yes.'

'And you to them. In fact, you quite got to know them. Now, I'm thinking of the Lady Irina in particular, because she was your special friend.'

'She sat me on her lap.'

'Well, that was nice.'

'And she smelled all sweet.'

'And you chatted away, I expect?'

'About the Sultan.'

'About the Sultan?' This was not quite what he had expected.

'Yes. She said he loved her but that she wasn't sure that he loved her enough. Sometimes she thought he didn't love her and that made her very unhappy. She said she wanted to be sure of him and would I help her.'

'But how could you help her?'

Chloe was silent for a moment. Then she said: 'It's a secret.'

'Ah, a secret, is it?'

'Yes. Between me and her.'

'Well, I'm not going to ask you what it is, then.'

'I wouldn't tell you. I wouldn't tell anybody.'

'Quite right. She had put her trust in you.'

'And it was a big trust. She told me that.'

'But you wouldn't let her down.'

'Never!' said Chloe firmly.

Seymour wondered how he could take this further.

'*You* wouldn't,' he said, 'but someone else might.'

'Someone else?'

'Well, you could hardly be expected to do this on your own.'

'I can do my bit on my own. And that's the important bit. She told me.'

'Yes, but after that? Can she rely on . . . the person who had to do the next bit?'

'She can rely on us,' said Chloe, 'absolutely.'

*   *   *

Seymour had no particular desire to do Stevens a favour. But while he was in the Embassy that evening ('Pop in for a drink, old man') he thought he might as well raise it.

'Been talking to Stevens,' he said. 'He wondered if you'd got wind of any rivals.'

'Rivals?'

'You know, for the sort of thing he's doing. Back-up facilities, and all that.'

'I would have thought one lot of maintenance facilities would be enough. Christ, it's only three machines. Is he afraid of losing the contract or something?'

Seymour told Farquhar about the cut cables.

'Phew, that's a bit vicious!' said Farquhar. 'If it *is* a rival.' He shook his head. 'But, no, we've not heard of anything. The closest we've come to it is Orhan Eser complaining.'

'Complaining? What's he complaining of?'

'The Blériot machines. He says it's destabilizing the international situation and we ought to do something about it. As if we could! But he raised it just in a general way. He's up here from time to time, you know, mainly to talk about things affecting the Sultan. But sometimes he raises other issues. Mostly to do with the war at the moment. I don't know whether he's for it or against it. Maybe he hopes that if there's a war and it goes badly for the Ottomans, then there might be a chance of the Sultan being brought back. You never can tell with Orhan. He plays his cards close to his chest. Of course, that could be because he hasn't got any.'

'Well, you wouldn't have many, would you?' said Seymour. 'Not if your only function in life is being part of the entourage of an exiled Sultan!'

Farquhar laughed.

'His only hope is of a turn-around. But that's not entirely out of the question. Things could hardly be said to be stable in Istanbul just at the moment.'

'But he was asking about the Blériot machines, you say?'

'In a very general way. Complaining about them, I suppose. I don't think he's as detached as he pretends, nor as out of politics as he lets on. I wouldn't be surprised if he's relaying information back to Istanbul, and the machines are part of it.'

'You think the Ottomans are worried about them?'

'No, I don't think so. Not really. They're more worried about the soldiers. Of course, they'd like to have some flying machines themselves. But they could be angling for someone to sell them some, so there could be a rival for Stevens in that sense. But, frankly, I don't think they've got the money just at the moment. Nor have the Greeks, of course, although that's not stopping them. But I don't think it's just that.'

'No?'

'No. The fact is, I just don't see it. The Ottomans with flying machines? They're different from the Greeks. Look, you've seen how it is in Athens. Everyone here is crazy about them. The young are queuing up to fly them. But the Ottomans are not like that. Half of them have never heard of a Blériot machine and the other half have but think it's just a Western lie. In the end it comes down to a difference of societies. And do you know where I think the difference lies?'

'No?'

'Sporting spirit.'

'What!'

'The Greeks have it, the Ottomans don't. The Greeks are like us. Think of motor cars. What do young chaps in England do as soon as they've got one?'

'Well, drive them, I suppose.'

'Race them. And the Greeks are like that. Go to the new Phaleron Road and what do you see? Bicyclists. Racing. And as soon as they've got cars, that's what they'll be doing with them. Do you ever see Ottomans racing on bicycles?'

'Well, no, but —'

'Well, there you are: lack of sporting spirit.'

114

'Yes, but –'

'Why do young Greeks take to the air?'

'Because a few have rich dads and –'

'There are rich dads in Istanbul. Why don't their sons want them to buy a Blériot?'

'I expect there are other things they want them to spend their money on.'

'Exactly! Whereas rich young men in England look at things like motor cars and Blériot machines and say, "Wow! How can we play with them?" Well, the Greeks are like that. And the Ottomans aren't. That's the difference between them. And that's why it would be no good the Ottomans buying flying machines. They wouldn't know what to do with them.'

'What about the war? If there is one. Stevens thinks –'

'Oh, Stevens!'

'You don't think it will make any difference? Having Blériot machines?'

'Absolutely none.'

Seymour did not know a lot about the diplomatic service. From what he had seen, in brief visits to Trieste and Istanbul and now Athens, British diplomats were a mixture of brilliance and battiness. When they were on international politics they were sometimes brilliant. But then there were the bicycle-racing Ottomans! And these were the guys who were trying to stop a Balkan war?

The idea that the young Greek flyers would sleep beside the Blériots had brought tension to the Metaxas household.

'Sleep?' Dr Metaxas had said. 'Or not sleep? Which is it to be? If sleep, you're not going to be much use as a guard. If not sleep, you're not going to be much use in classes next day.'

Andreas had replied hotly that the Blériots were more

115

important than classes. This had upset both his parents: his father because he thought that education was more important than flying and that Andreas had cut enough classes already, his mother because she was so opposed to war anyway. Stevens had attempted to calm her fears by saying hastily that there was no question of Andreas getting involved in the war. All they were talking about was guarding the Blériot machines.

'And after?' Mrs Metaxas had said.

'If Andreas flies at all,' Stevens had said, 'and George, too,' he had added, turning to George's parents, 'it will be for purposes of general reconnaissance only. Aerial warfare will be left to the professional flyers when they arrive.'

This had not pleased Andreas or George, who had had far more exciting things in mind, and not convinced either Dr Metaxas or his wife.

'It would hardly even be reconnaissance,' Stevens had said. 'Call it just taking a look-around.'

'Yes, but do the Ottomans know the difference?' Dr Metaxas had asked; and Mrs Metaxas had pursed her lips.

This was all very unfortunate as Andreas had invited Stevens to dinner in the hope that he would persuade them about his flying activities. He had also invited George and his parents. This, he had thought, was a cunning move, since George's mother had been a friend of Mrs Metaxas since schooldays and could normally be relied on to support their cause.

He had overlooked, however, the fact that Dr Metaxas didn't get on particularly well with George's mother, whom he regarded as a foolish woman who spoiled her son, and absolutely detested George's father, whom he saw as a rapacious businessman. To make matters worse, George's father looked on the Blériot he had bought his son as an investment to be protected and was all in favour of mounting the guard.

'It will keep the machines in the air,' said Andreas, pleased.

'What a pity!' said his father: and the rest of the evening, said Aphrodite, had gone like that.

The evening had had, however, from Seymour's point of view, some good consequences. In a valiant attempt to retrieve the dinner, George's mother had asked Aphrodite about her plans for when she left university. Aphrodite had said that she would need to get some hospital experience before really deciding and that she had thought of going to England to get it. This was news to Dr Metaxas and news at which his heart brightened. Did it mean that Aphrodite was going, after all, to stick to medicine and abandon her plans for a future repairing Blériot machines?

Hardly daring to hope, he had said that England was a good place to gain medical experience and that there were some good training hospitals in London: St Bartholomew's, for instance.

Aphrodite, not wishing to make it too easy for her father, had been doubtful. The place sounded religious, and she didn't think religion and medicine mixed, as they were too inclined to do in Greece.

'Religious?' said Seymour, to whom she was recounting this afterwards.

'Saints,' said Aphrodite. 'St Bartholomew's. It sounds a churchy place to me.'

Seymour, who knew Bart's and its students, said that he didn't think there were too many saints in the place or priests and that he had never seen much evidence of any religious connection.

A rather greater problem was that he hadn't seen many women there, either; at least, not as doctors.

This was serious and they spent a surprisingly long time discussing it next day as they sat having a coffee in Constitution Square. Seymour said he would look into it when he got back and that then, perhaps, Aphrodite could come and study the situation for herself.

Chapter Eight

Seymour checked back through the prescriptions until he found the one Dr Metaxas had made out for the Lady Irina. Then he took it to an apothecary.

'Could you tell me, please, what this might be prescribed for?'

The apothecary took one look at it and handed it back.

'Constipation,' he said.

'And it's powerful, is it?'

The apothecary took back the paper.

'In the doses written, here, yes. It certainly is. Very.'

'Thank you.'

Seymour went to the Sultan's house and asked to see the Lady Irina.

A little later she appeared, veiled, as before, and with the attendant eunuch.

'Would you tell the Lady Irina that I am glad to see she has recovered.'

'Recovered?'

'From her affliction.'

'Affliction?'

'The one that prompted her to seek the doctor's help.'

'Oh, that, yes. Yes, thank you. I have recovered.'

She has recovered, translated the eunuch. Needlessly, since she spoke in French and Seymour understood perfectly. However, the decencies were preserved.

'I am asking because I gather the medicine was very powerful. *Formidable*, was, I think, the description someone used. And yet it seems to have had no effect on the Lady Irina.'

There was a little pause.

'The Lady Irina has a strong constitution.'

'Yes, I'm sure. I just wondered if she had, in fact, taken it.'

'Certainly she took it.'

'*She* took it? And not someone else?'

The eunuch hesitated.

'I am not sure what the Effendi means.'

'I think the Lady Irina may understand.'

The Lady Irina laughed.

'Yes,' she said, 'the Lady Irina understands.'

'And did someone else take it?'

'It is possible.'

'With such a formidable medicine, the effects could be severe.'

'They certainly could,' said the Lady Irina. 'Especially if the dosage were doubled or trebled.'

'Thank you, Lady Irina. All is now clear.'

But how was he to use it? He tried it out first on Orhan Eser.

'I think it possible,' he said cautiously, 'that His Royal Highness's sufferings may not have been due to poisoning but to his having inadvertently taken a very powerful laxative.'

'Nonsense!' said Orhan Eser. 'He was poisoned!'

'I have reason to think that was not the case.'

Orhan Eser snorted. 'Surely the doctors –'

'Have found no evidence of poisoning. Nor have the laboratory analyses.'

'There is some doubt about this –'

'But on the whole the consensus is that he was not

119

poisoned. And it appears that a strong laxative was passed into the harem.'

'His Highness would certainly not have taken it unless one of his doctors had prescribed it.'

'But I think he may not have known he was taking it.'

'It was disguised, you mean?'

'Well, possibly.'

'Then someone must have disguised it! This is very disquieting. In view of what happened to the cat. You are confirming that there is a poisoner at work –'

'No, no. Not exactly. Not exactly a poisoner –'

'It sounds very like one to me. An attempt on His Highness's life –'

'Well, hardly. If what I am supposing is correct.'

'It is, at the very least, an assault on His Royal Highness's *person*. I shall have to report this to the Acting-Vizier.'

Abd-es-Salaam listened intently.

'You are saying that the Sultan has unwittingly taken a strong laxative and that this accounts for his stomach pains?'

'Could account, yes.'

'And that someone – if I understand Orhan Eser correctly – consciously gave it him?'

'I think so, yes.'

'But this is very disquieting! An assault on His Highness's person –'

'I thought, sir, that you would be relieved to know that it *wasn't* a case of poisoning.'

'But it could so easily have been. Does it not confirm that there is someone at work? Behind our defences? Cold-bloodedly trying out how best to –'

'I don't think that is necessarily so, sir.'

'First, the cat. Then –'

'I don't think the two cases are necessarily related, sir.'

'You mean that there are *two* poisoners at work? *Two*?'

'No, no, no . . .'

In the end Seymour succeeded in persuading the Acting-Vizier that since this was a case only of suspicion, it would be best if it were left to him to pursue his enquiries. He didn't want heads to roll prematurely. Heads to roll? He hoped that was a figure of speech.

'Had the same sort of problem myself!' said the First Secretary sympathetically.

'Problem?'

'Constipation. It's the oil. You see, in England they use fat –'

'Yes, yes. My point is that I don't think the Powers should worry about poisoning.'

'Just a laxative gone wrong?'

'That's right.'

'But – if I follow you – someone gave him the laxative? Isn't that rather a hostile act?'

'More of a joke, I think.'

Seymour was sitting in the square having a coffee with Aphrodite. She was supposed to be on her way to the university but was in no hurry and was telling him about the dinner party the previous evening when Andreas, Stevens and George sat down at a table not far away. After a moment Andreas caught Aphrodite's eye. He looked away immediately, disconcerted. Aphrodite seemed slightly disconcerted, too.

Andreas got up and came across to them.

'Aren't you supposed to be going to the university?' he said.

'Yes,' said Aphrodite. 'Aren't you?'

This clearly posed a problem to Andreas.

'I'm on my way,' he said.

'Me, too.'

Andreas lingered. Seymour suddenly realized that he

was off-put by seeing his sister sitting unchaperoned with Seymour. Despite his zeal for the modern, for Blériot machines, at any rate, he was still in some ways an unreconstructed Greek male.

After a while, as Aphrodite showed no sign of moving, he went back to join the others.

Aphrodite, however, despite her victory, seemed uncomfortable and a moment or two later, with a slightly ill grace, she got to her feet. Relaxed though the behaviour of the Metaxas family was by Greek standards, they tended, as Seymour had already seen, to keep one another in line.

A little later, Andreas, equally reluctantly, got up from his table too and followed after her. George, showing sympathetic male solidarity with his classmate, went with him. Stevens, however, who had risen with them, came across to where Seymour was sitting.

'Mind if I join you?'

'Please do.'

'I need your help,' said Stevens. 'The fact is, I've buggered things up. With the Metaxases: I know you're a friend of the family and maybe you can help me to put things right.'

'Well, of course, anything I can do . . .'

'Nice people. It's Andreas I know best, of course. I like him a lot. He took me over to their place yesterday evening. He's been having some difficulties, I gather, and he thought I could help him.'

'Oh, yes?'

'I don't think I did,' said Stevens, with refreshing honesty. 'In fact, I think I may have made things worse.'

'How was that?'

'We-ell, I think his parents are a bit bothered by the flying. People often are, especially parents. They think it's dangerous. It's not, of course, not if you do it properly. One thing it is, though, is expensive, and I can understand it if they have misgivings about that, as, I gather, Dr Metaxas has. But I think I can take care of that. See Andreas gets a flight from time to time. George is very generous and I can get the others to let him have a go, too. And maybe when the new machines come . . .

'But that, actually, is not really the problem. Nor, in a general way, is it the safety. It's the war business. Mrs Metaxas especially.'

He gave Seymour a quick glance.

'You know about this? No? Andreas told me. And, I must say, after that I could understand . . .

'Well, apparently, as a child she got mixed up in one of these wars that are forever going on in the Balkans. I think this one was something to do with Bulgaria. I remember my father speaking about it, he had been to some big meeting, at which Gladstone had spoken. "Bulgarian horrors," I think Gladstone had said. I don't remember the details. Russia was involved. And Serbia – Serbia is always involved, isn't it, in something like this? Anyway, they were driving the Muslims out, and the Ottomans turned nasty and started massacring the Christians – you can work it out, can't you, and guess what went on.

'There were lots of little ethnic groups, peoples, who fell between all the stools and so got it in the neck from all sides. One of them was the Vlachs. They live up in the mountains mostly and are Christian, only a different sort of Christianity from the Russian sort and the Bulgarian sort. They went in for the Greek sort, which was a big mistake since they got hammered by everyone else, Russians, Bulgarians, Ottomans, Serbs.

'The Greeks went in to help them, and one of those Greeks was a young doctor named Metaxas. One day he went into a Vlach village which had just been visited by – well, I don't know which of them it was. And he found a young girl, fifteen, she was, and – Look, I don't think I want to tell you what he found, you can imagine. Well, the young girl was Mrs Metaxas, he took her home to

Greece and married her. And since that time I think you can guess how she feels about wars.

'And I respect those feelings. I do. Really. And I can understand how she feels about her son. I've got kids of my own back in London and I'd feel exactly the same. So I'm going to keep him out of it. Fly, yes, but fight, no. Leave that to the professionals. He's got to fly, he'll go mad if he doesn't, but I'll see he gets nowhere near the front line. Reconnaissance, let's call it reconnaissance, yes, but it'll be this side of the mountains. And I'll go with him. But that's all it will be.

'Now, I want you to tell Mrs Metaxas that, because when I spoke I got it wrong. I'm not good at talking, machines are more my line, and I put my foot in it. Now, I couldn't bear to hurt that lady, not after what she's been through. Andreas told me all about it and I've not been able to get it out of my mind. I'm not just an ignorant technician, you know. So you tell her. Please. Set her mind at rest. Tell her I'll keep him away from it all if anything starts.

'If I can. Because that's another thing. The boy has got a mind of his own. He's mad keen to be part of any action. They all are. In a way it's fine, it's how young men should be. But I know how she feels. So you'll tell her, will you? You're in with the family, I've seen you with the girl. You tell her, will you?'

The results of the analysis of the medicines prescribed for the ladies of the harem had been promised him for later that afternoon. This was so speedy that he hadn't really believed it. Things did not work like that in London! Nevertheless, the people in the laboratories had been so confident that he walked across there after his siesta, and, to his surprise, they were ready.

They showed nothing untoward. The medicines were as the prescriptions said they should be and there was no question of any of them being a poison in disguise. Seymour had not really expected otherwise, but it had been necessary to check. Only one or two of the medicines had not been traced – used up, those for whom they had been prescribed claimed. The most notable of these was the laxative prescribed for Irina and Seymour was pretty sure he knew what had happened to that.

The poison which had killed the cat had passed into the harem by some other means. Although Orhan Eser and the eunuchs had been confident that nothing could get into the harem without their knowledge, Seymour had learned that there were loopholes. Medicine, possibly; but if not medicine then potions of another kind.

He went back to the Sultan's house. It was between meals and he found Amina ensconced, dozing, in her cubby-hole.

'Amina,' said Seymour, 'you are one who has seen all. You have seen the great fall and the humble rise.'

'I have,' agreed the old woman happily.

'And I admire you,' said Seymour. 'For you have remained true in adversity. The Sultan's adversity.'

'I have,' agreed Amina, 'and that cannot be said of many.'

'Tell me, how is it that you stayed with the Sultan when so many left? For – forgive me, Amina, I do not wish to offend – you work here in a lowly position. There are Greeks here who could do your work as well as you, or people from the mountains.'

'That girl, Chloe,' spat Amina venomously. 'Although she will never to able to do what I do. Try as I might, I cannot teach her orderliness, discipline. But it is true what you say: the Sultan could not bring many with him and so he has been obliged to fill his service with the lowest of the low: Greeks. Greeks from the sewers of Salonica and the cesspits of Athens.'

'And from the mountains,' said Seymour.

'Vlachs,' said Amina. 'You can't get lower than that.'

'And yet, since the Sultan could not bring many, it was right not to bring kitchen servants from Istanbul. So how did it come about that he brought you?'

125

'Oh, I wasn't in the kitchen. I was in the harem.'

'So you have told me. But – forgive me again – how does it come about that you are in the kitchens now?'

'The Sultan would not take me. "It is a small harem now," he said, "and those who serve in it must be found locally. Except for the eunuchs, for where will we find them except in Istanbul?"'

'Then . . .?'

'It was Abd-es-Salaam. He said, "Let me take Amina, for she is wise in the ways of the harem." But the Sultan said, "She is too old. She has served her time. Let her now go back to her village." But the people in the village did not want me back. They said, "It is many years since she was here and no one knows her now. Besides she is trouble-some." And they went to Abd-es-Salaam – he had been our Pasha once, so they knew him – and told him this.

'And Abd-es-Salaam went to the Sultan and said, "She has served us well; let us keep her." But the Sultan said, "Look, if I can take only a few of my wives, I am certainly not taking a servant of over eighty!" But Abd-es-Salaam said, "She will be useful to us. She keeps her ear to the ground and tells me what she hears. It is a help to me in managing the harem."

'But still the Sultan said no. So Abd-es-Salaam called me and said, "Amina, if you came with us, it can only be as the lowest of servants." "Nevertheless, I will go with you," I said. So he found space for me in one of the wagons and when we got to Salonica he told Orhan Eser to take me on in the kitchen. But Orhan Eser did not know me from Istanbul days and he said, "She is too old. She will not be able to do the work." But Abd-es-Salaam said, "There are different kinds of work and different ways of doing it." So Orhan Eser did as Abd-es-Salaam bade him. And it was as well, for he was filling the place with Vlachs and such people and none of them knew how work in the harem should be done.'

'Then it was indeed as well that you were there,' said

Seymour, 'for it is not right that the old standards should be let slip.'

'It is bad enough anyway,' said Amina, looking round her with a shudder. 'What sort of place is this for a palace?'

'Not much of one, truly,' said Seymour. 'And yet the life of the harem goes on.'

'It goes on,' agreed Amina.

'Much as it always has done?'

'Much as it always has done.' Amina gave a sudden cackle. 'For it is about the same things as it always was.'

'Men and women. There you have it,' said Seymour. 'It always was thus and always will be.'

'Men and women,' repeated Amina. 'You can't alter that and you never will be able to.'

'And my guess is,' said Seymour '– but you are wise in this and I am not – that they are still up to their old tricks.'

The old woman smirked.

'Always were and always will be,' she muttered.

'Always seeking to get round the rules,' suggested Seymour.

'They have to be kept down,' said the old woman, with sudden vehemence. 'Once the rules are let slip, order is gone.'

Her mind began to wander.

'Order . . .' she muttered. 'Discipline. That's what they need. That's what is needed nowadays. That girl . . . no standards.'

'Which girl is this?'

'That Chloe. Needs to be kept up to the mark . . .'

She was becoming tired. He knew he would have to catch her before she faded completely.

'And not just her,' he prompted. 'There are those within the harem –'

'There are,' she agreed.

'– who look outward –'

Unexpectedly, she demurred.

127

'Not much chance of that,' she said. 'The walls of the harem still hold.'

'There is no dalliance?'

'They wish there were!'

'But there is not. How comes it, then, that potions pass to and fro?'

'Potions?'

'Love potions. You told me yourself.'

'Po . . .' Her head nodded.

'Potions,' said Seymour sharply. 'Love potions.'

She snapped awake.

'Love potions.' She laughed. 'There are always those.'

'Who for? Who asks for love potions?'

'They all do.' She laughed again. 'They fight,' she said admiringly. 'Like cocks in a yard.'

'For the Sultan's favour?'

'Oh, yes,' she said drowsily, beginning to slip away again.

He made one last desperate effort.

'Who from? Who do they get them from, Amina?'

He had a sudden realization.

'Not you, Amina?'

She cackled.

'They ask,' she said. 'They ask old Amina. Who knows all.'

'And you make them?'

She snapped up again, affronted.

'I?' she said. 'What do you think I am? I, who have lived in the palace for more than fifty years? What should I know of such arts?'

'Then . . .?'

'These are dark arts. And people who know them. Not fit . . . Not fit to work in a palace. Backward. Dirty! That girl, Chloe.'

She was back on her old obsession again. His heart sank.

'It is a dark business,' he agreed, 'making love potions.

And dark people who know it. But who in the palace knows such people?'

She seemed puzzled.

'Who . . .?'

'The potions. Who supplies them?'

'The dark people.' She seemed surprised. 'I have told you. Backward. We wouldn't have had them in the old days. They are the ones who know about such things.'

'The people of the hills?' he guessed.

'Dirty! That girl, Chloe.'

'But she, surely –'

Amina shook her head impatiently.

'Not her,' she said. 'But she knows. They come right into the palace. These days.'

Her head nodded down.

'Amina.'

The eyes opened.

'They fight,' she said. 'Like cocks in a yard. Always have done. For his favour.'

She cackled.

'Love potions!' she said. 'And not just the women, either.'

Seymour stood there for some time waiting to see if she rallied again, but she didn't. He heard little snores. He was going to get no more out of Amina.

She had told him quite a lot, however, some of it surprising and which opened new doors. That last remark of hers: not just the women. She must mean the eunuchs. But – love potions?

In the kitchen they were just starting to prepare the evening meal. They were not so busy yet, however, as not to be able to offer him a strong cup of black tea, and were quite happy to stand around chatting while he sipped it.

'Where have you been, then?'

'The harem.' He shook his head. 'Funny place, that.'

'You're telling me!'

129

'And those eunuchs!'

'Funny people,' they agreed.

'Wouldn't want it, myself.'

'Of course, it was done to them when they were too young to know any better,' someone said. 'While they were still children.'

'Can't understand that,' said someone else. 'Would you give your children away like that to be . . .?'

'You might if you were dirt poor. I mean, you might see it as a good thing for them.'

'Yes, but – I mean, you've got to think about them, haven't you? Having that done would cut you off from – I mean, for life . . .'

'Yes, but suppose you were so poor that you knew they'd never be able to marry? If that was the way you could see it was going to be, you might think your children would be better off in a harem. At least you wouldn't starve, would you? And it's not a bad life. They do all right, those eunuchs.'

'Sit on their backsides all day.'

'Just watching the women. Come to think of it, I wouldn't mind doing that myself.'

'You'd get fed up with it.'

'Not for quite a while. But it's true that then I might feel the need for other amusements.'

'But that's just what you wouldn't be able to have, see, not if you had been –'

'*Do* the eunuchs here have other amusements?' asked Seymour. 'I ask as one who is ignorant.'

There was some debate about this.

'You see I was wondering about His Highness. If his tastes extended to – well, you know, wider than women.'

'Not from what I've heard.'

That seemed to be the general consensus.

'You wouldn't need it, would you, not with all those women.'

'Yes, but I was just wondering if his tastes maybe inclined in that direction.'

But they didn't think so; and on matters like this Seymour was inclined to trust the kitchen's opinion.

Not the Sultan's favours, then. But possibly among the eunuchs themselves . . .?

'Lady Samira, I have been thinking about the harem as a place. No doubt it is somewhere where there are great passions loose –'

'Oh, there are, there are!'

'And not all of them are focused, as they should be, on His Highness?'

'It's true we hate each other,' said Samira, after a moment's reflection.

'Love, too?'

'Love?' Samira seemed astonished. 'Oh, I know what you mean. Well, there's a little of that, of course. You could hardly expect it to be otherwise. But less than you might suppose. The Sultan doesn't like the thought of sharing his favours and Abd-es-Salaam is rather strict about it. And, of course, the eunuchs run to him immediately there is a suspicion –don't they, Talal?'

'We do our duty,' muttered Talal.

'And what about the eunuchs themselves?' asked Seymour. 'Do they never dote on one of the royal ladies?'

'*What*!' said Samira.

'Never!' cried Talal.

'But, surely, seeing such beauty –'

'But they're eunuchs!' cried Samira.

'So they never seek a lady's smile?'

'The only smile they would get would be a pitying one,' said Samira.

'Maybe, but –'

'Never!' said Talal firmly. 'Not even a pitying one. It would be more than our life would be worth.'

'I do see that. But, Talal, to be forever excluded from the

world of passion, as well, of course, from the physical possibility, seems to me unjust. But perhaps you are not excluded from the world of passion?'

'Of course he is excluded!' said Samira. 'Poor man!'

'But are there not friendships among the eunuchs themselves?' asked Seymour.

Talal thought.

'We hang together,' he said. 'And get on well.'

'Oh, I know what you're asking,' said Samira excitedly, clapping her hands. 'I'd never thought of that. Talal, do you have a grand passion for Ali? Or Hassan? Come on, do tell us!'

'I certainly don't,' said Talal stuffily.

'Well, I can understand that,' said Samira. 'One look at Ali should be enough. But what,' she said roguishly, 'about the other way? Does Ali have a grand passion for you, Talal?'

'We don't go in for that sort of thing,' said Talal firmly. 'And now, Lady Samira, it is time you returned to your apartments.'

'Oh, but we haven't started. I want to talk about passion with Mr Seymour. This is beginning quite promisingly. Have you ever experienced a grand passion, Mr Seymour? Or perhaps you *are* experiencing it.'

'I think perhaps I can feel one coming on,' said Seymour.

Samira clapped her hands again.

'There you are, Talal! How exciting! Now, Mr Seymour –'

'This way!' said Talal.

It had been the only way he could see of doing it and now he was not sure how much he could rely on what he had found out. Maybe not the eunuchs; but if not the eunuchs, who, then?

*   *   *

The next morning Seymour was having breakfast and wondering as usual why, with oranges all round them, the Greeks couldn't make decent marmalade, when there was a commotion outside the door and Farquhar burst into the dining room.

'Seymour! Thank goodness I've found you! You've got to come at once.'

'What's the matter?' said Seymour, getting to his feet.

'Stevens. He's dead.'

Chapter Nine

'Dead!' And then, as thoughts flooded in: 'The Blériot?'

'Yes.'

'Anyone with him?'

'There was a young chap.'

Andreas. It must be Andreas.

'This morning?'

'Yes.'

He felt sickened.

'Both of them?'

'No, no. Just Stevens.'

'How's Metaxas?'

'Metaxas?'

'The other chap.'

'He's all right. Shocked, of course.'

'He was lucky.'

'Lucky?'

'To get out alive. People usually don't.'

'What are you talking about?'

'The crash.'

'Crash? There wasn't one.'

'Then what –'

'They got back safely. In the ordinary way. It was only then that they found – Stevens was in the seat behind, you see. The young chap didn't know.'

For a moment he had feared – the cut cables had come into his mind.

'Just Stevens, then?'

'Yes.'

'Heart attack?'

Farquhar was silent for a moment. Then:

'He was poisoned,' he said.

Andreas was sitting on the ground beside the Blériot, his head in his hands. The mechanics were standing there silently. Two Greek policemen were waiting nearby and there was another man, with a smiley face, not in uniform, a detective, probably. Seymour went across and introduced himself.

The detective looked at him in surprise.

'You speak Greek? Of course! You must be the man they've sent out from Scotland Yard.' The smiley face crinkled into a definite smile. 'To investigate a murder. Of a cat!'

'Not my idea,' said Seymour hastily.

'No, I'll bet!' He held out his hand. 'Konstantin Popadopoulos. People call me Pop.'

He shook hands too with Farquhar, whom he seemed to know.

'Sorry to see you, Mr Farquhar, on such an occasion. But glad to see you in another way. Perhaps you could help us? I need to visit Mr Stevens' flat and would prefer you to be there.'

'Glad to see you, Pop,' said Farquhar. 'Of course I'll come round with you. Pleased it's you and not someone else.'

A carriage was just coming round the side of the buildings. It had a long, boxlike compartment and there were no windows.

Popadopoulos put his hand on Andreas's shoulder.

'You must get up now, Mr Metaxas,' he said, firmly but kindly.

Andreas rose obediently.

'Take him inside, will you?' he said to the mechanics. 'Give him some coffee.'

They led him away.

135

'It is best, perhaps, if he does not see what happens next,' Popadopoulos said. 'We have to get the body out of the cockpit and I am afraid it may be stiff.'

The carriage was drawing up. Its rear doors opened. Two men emerged carrying a stretcher.

'Do you want to see?' Popadopoulos asked Seymour. He took him over to the Blériot. Stevens was slumped in the cockpit. Someone had undone the helmet.

'They thought it might be shortage of oxygen,' said Popadopoulos. 'But then they smelt –'

The face was disfigured.

'Not much doubt about the cause,' said the Greek.

The stretcher-bearers looked at him questioningly.

The detective nodded.

One of the bearers climbed up on the fuselage and put his hands under Stevens' armpits.

After a short struggle they managed to get him out and laid him on the stretcher. Popadopoulos bent over the body for a moment and studied it. Then he glanced at the stretcher-bearers.

'Okay,' he said.

They lifted the stretcher into the carriage and closed the door.

Popadopoulos turned to the mechanics.

'So,' he said conversationally, 'what would he have done when he got here this morning? Just take me through.'

'Well, he was going out early, with Mr Metaxas. And he wanted the machine to be ready, so he worked on it himself.' The mechanic looked at him. '*Very* early,' he said. 'Before, in the normal way, we would have got here. Petras offered to come in, but he said no, he'd do it himself.'

'What would he have done?'

'Checks, mostly. He knew we'd given the engine a good going over the day before when it had got back, so he would have just done the routine checks, ignition, fuel, controls, that sort of thing.'

'Cables?' said Seymour.

'He'd have checked them in the normal way. There are

procedures you go through. Mr Stevens was meticulous about them. He insisted we follow the routine. Not just us, but the pilots, too. We had to go through them in the same way. Every time. "Go through them," he would say, "until they're automatic. Until you don't even have to think."'

'So he would have done that, too?'

'"If you do it wrong, I shall bawl you out," he would say. "And if I do it wrong, I expect you to bawl me out. There are no short cuts in this sort of thing."'

'So everything was in order, then?'

'The machine came back, didn't it?'

'Look, it wasn't the machine,' said another of the mechanics. 'He was poisoned!'

'Yes, I know. I'm just getting a picture of what happened this morning. So he went through the tests and when he had finished them, he sat down and waited for Mr Metaxas?'

'He wouldn't have had to wait long. He was already here.'

'Already here?'

'Sleeping beneath the machine.'

'Sleeping beneath the –?' said Popadopoulos, amazed. 'Doesn't he have a bed to go to?'

'It was to guard the machines,' said Seymour.

'Guard the –?'

'There was an attack on them. Some cables were cut.'

'So we agreed to mount guard. We would take it in turns. the young men, too.'

'When you say "cut" –'

'Deliberately.'

'But this is very interesting!' cried Popadopoulos. 'What you are saying is that there was an earlier attack? Before the one on Mr Stevens?'

'That's right, yes.'

'The cables are important, yes? It could have resulted in someone's death?'

'If Nico hadn't spotted it.'

'I couldn't believe my eyes! I went home and told Maria –'

'Yes, yes. And presumably you told Mr Stevens?'

'Too true, I did. Pretty quickly! "Look," I said, "look at this! Tell me if that's an accident!" Well, he only needed to take one look. "That's not an accident," he said. "I've seen this once before."'

'It could not have been a mistake? While someone was working?'

'Mistake? Listen, you don't make a mistake like that. Not if you're a proper mechanic, and everyone here is. It was cut, I tell you! Cut! Deliberately.'

'You are saying that there was a definite intention –'

'To bloody kill someone! When I told Maria, she said, "There's a nutter around. I hope you weren't thinking of going up in one of those machines yourself!" "It's not my job to test-fly," I said. "And Mr Stevens is making damn sure that no one else goes up, either. Not until we've gone over the machines with a fine-tooth comb!"'

'We've started mounting a guard.'

'And that's what Mr Metaxas was doing?'

'It was his turn and –'

'Yes, yes.' Popadopoulos thought for a moment.

'Now, tell me, please: the cables were cut on one of the flying machines? Just one, yes? And was this the one that Mr Stevens was going to fly in?'

'You don't know which one he's going to fly in. He might go up with anybody.'

'Ah! So the attack was aimed not at him personally but at the machines in general?'

'You could say that, I suppose, yes. It looks that way.'

'It's important, you see.'

'Well, whichever way it was, it was aimed at him the next time.'

'I wonder,' said Popadopoulos.

Andreas was drinking coffee in a cubby-hole at the back of

the workshop. Popadopoulos put a hand sympathetically on his shoulder.

'Don't get up,' he said. He perched himself on a stool opposite him. 'This has been a great shock, I know, and I don't want to make things worse. But there are some questions I have to ask you.'

'Of course,' said Andreas.

'You found out, I gather, only after you had landed?'

'That's right, yes. I got out of the cockpit and turned to speak to him and then, when he did not reply, I looked closer.'

'And then?'

'Called Vasco.'

'A mechanic?'

'Yes. And then the others came. And they couldn't believe it, and I couldn't believe it. Someone unstrapped his helmet. We thought he maybe needed air . . . But then we saw . . . I couldn't believe it!'

'Of course not. Of course not. And you had not had an inkling? There had been nothing during the flight, to make you suppose . . .?'

'Nothing!'

'Do you communicate? While you're flying?'

'You can't really hear. It he wanted something, he would tap me on the shoulder and point.'

'And did he do this? On this flight?'

'I think so, yes. Once or twice. When we got close to the mountains. He pointed out our army below.'

'And this would have been – about halfway through the flight, say?'

'About two thirds of the way. I wondered if he wanted me to go over the mountains. You know, to take a look at the other side. To see what the enemy were doing.'

'Enemy?'

'The Ottomans.'

'But he indicated that he didn't want that?'

'That's right. I just pointed, of course. But he didn't seem to –'

'Did he seem all right when you had this exchange?'

'Yes. Yes, I think so.'

Andreas hesitated.

'I think perhaps he may have been feeling cold. He had some coffee. He offered me some but I didn't want any. I don't when I'm flying.'

'But he did?'

'Yes. I thought it may have been to warm himself up. I suppose I had gone a bit higher – in case he wanted me to cross the mountains. I think that may have made him feel cold, because he asked me again, a little later. He touched me on the back and held out the flask to me. But I didn't want it, I shook my head.

'But he was insistent, he held it out to me again, touched me with it. But I really didn't want any. I pushed it away. I was concentrating on flying.'

'I see. And then?'

'He gave up. Sat back.'

'And the flask?'

'Flask?'

'What happened to the flask?'

'He took it back, I suppose.'

'You didn't notice anything unusual? At that point?'

'No. Absolutely not. I didn't notice anything until . . .'

'Mr Farquhar!' cried Popadopoulos with concern. 'I have kept you waiting!'

'That's all right,' said Farquhar amicably. 'You've got your job to do.'

'And you've got yours! Come, let us go. And Mr Seymour, too! May I borrow your carriage? There is room for me, too? A little one, just a little one. You can squeeze me into a corner. There! Yes? Everyone comfortable? And tell me, Mr Farquhar, how is the Ambassador? Keeping well, I hope?'

Stevens had lived in lodgings within walking distance of his workshop, so they didn't have far to go. According to his landlady, another of those animated ladies dressed all in black, this had suited him because he had worked all hours. Often he did not get back until late at night, especially recently when the private Blériots had been flying all the time and he had been helping with their servicing.

'Work was everything to him,' the landlady said approvingly.

But then she added, less approvingly, 'Athens, nothing.'

By this she seemed to mean that unlike most of the visitors who came to stay in her house, he had shown no interest in the famous sites of the city. The Parthenon, the Acropolis, might never have existed as far as he was concerned. With decent Athenian pride, she found this slightly shocking.

Until recently, when 'the boys' had started taking him, he had hardly ever gone into the town. No restaurants, no bars, no late nights. This was, perhaps, as it should be, for he was a married man with a family in England. They could see the photograph in his room, and a lovely family they looked. All the same, it was a little surprising. But then, he cared passionately for his machines, said the landlady, laughing; and maybe it was better to care for them than for some of the ladies you met in Athens nowadays!

'And this morning?' prompted Popadopoulos patiently.

He had left early. Earlier even than usual. He was going to fly himself, he had told her, and he had wanted to prepare the machine. The mechanics would no doubt have done it but he hadn't wanted to get them in early because, after all, they had families too.

And what about breakfast, Popadopoulos asked?

Breakfast?

Had he had breakfast before leaving?

Well, yes, but . . .

The fact was that this was a bit of a sore point. She would willingly have prepared it for him but the thing was, you see, that he insisted on having porridge and, after the first week, had insisted, too, on preparing it

141

himself. This was no reflection on her, he had assured her: it was just that his mother and wife were Scottish and no one could make porridge like the Scots. And this skill had passed to him, he explained, sucked in with his mother's milk.

Milk, said Seymour: had he made his porridge with milk?

What, said the landlady?

The porridge: made with milk? Or water?

That, it turned out, was another vexed point. Stevens had spurned the milk she offered. There had, indeed, been words about it. What was wrong with her milk, she had demanded? The milk of Athens? Well, that was just the point. It tasted funny, or, at any rate, different from the milk he was used to. Perhaps it was the grass the cows fed upon.

Grass? Cows? There wasn't any grass in Athens; or cows, either.

For Christ's sake! Where did it come from, then? Goats? Bloody hell – forgive him, Madame! – that explained it. He would go for water.

Even about that there was some difficulty. The water, too, tasted differently from that in England.

That was because it was better, the landlady had said, beginning to bridle. It was pure. It came from the mountains. Did the water of England come from the mountains?

Not much: but in Scotland –

Mountain water, however, was acceptable and he had made his porridge with it: the best water, she pointed out firmly to Seymour and Farquhar.

Popadopoulos asked to see the oats Stevens made his porridge from and then folded some up in a little wisp of paper, which made the landlady begin to bridle again.

She had led them up to his room, where they had admired the photograph and Farquhar had begun to make a list of Stevens' effects. Popadopoulos had poked around the room but without finding anything, it seemed, worthy of his attention. Except –

142

There was bread on the table, and fruit. Popadopoulos slipped some of both into his pocket.

'Hey!' said the landlady. 'What do you think you're doing?'

'For analysis,' Popadopoulos explained hastily.

'There's nothing wrong with *my* bread.'

Farquhar said he would finish his list-making and then would go back to the workshop and pick up Andreas and take him home. Popadopoulos thanked the landlady profusely and announced that he would stroll back to the base. From the way he looked at Seymour, Seymour could see that he was meant to come, too.

'We are reproducing the walk that Stevens made,' he explained. 'If only for purposes of elimination.'

They passed a couple of bars, into which he stuck his nose and where he asked a question or two; but they did not detain him. Then they came to a bigger one where people were sitting having coffee and the patron was propped against the door.

Popadopoulos greeted him warmly and they sat down at a table.

'Your friend?' answered the patron, as he brought them the coffee. 'Yes. Every morning! As regular as clockwork.'

'But not this morning,' suggested Popadopoulos.

'No,' agreed the patron. 'He was a bit earlier this morning. I was still sweeping out.'

'And did he stop for anything? A cup of coffee, perhaps?'

'No,' said the patron. 'I don't understand these Englishmen. Why don't they take their breakfast on their way to work as everyone else does?'

He bent down over the table.

'Perhaps he's too big,' he whispered confidentially. 'You know who he is, of course?'

'Tell me.'

'He's in with the people at the base. The army. Got a

workshop there for those flying machines, the Blériots, you know. They say they wouldn't fly without him.'

'Really?'

'Yes, really.' The patron laid his finger alongside his nose. 'He's big. You mightn't think it, to look at him. But he's big with those Blériots.'

Popadopoulos sighed.

'You have heard, I expect,' he said gloomily, after the patron had gone, 'of the Great Athenian Love Affair? Our passion for flying machines?'

'I had noticed it, yes,' said Seymour.

'Everyone here is crazy about flying machines. Men, women, children, silver-haired matrons, grey-bearded dotards – everyone! It touches something deep inside us. It is the great Greek obsession. Like the Italian obsession with motor cars. Every Greek dreams of flying. Children wake up every morning and look behind their shoulder-blades to see if by chance they have sprouted wings over-night. People at the tables in Constitution Square sit with their eyes turned perpetually heavenwards.

'Even the politicians have got in on the act. "Vote for me and buy yourself a Blériot." And, of course, they do vote for them and the Government does buy Blériots.

'Only Athenians have got the myth wrong. They think they're Daedalus flying over the ocean but they're not; they're Tantalus pushing a great rock up a mountain, because Blériots have to be paid for and that means yet more taxes. Is your Government buying Blériots?'

'I don't think so.'

'Very sensible of them.'

'Stevens thought they should.'

'Ah, well, Stevens.'

He sipped his coffee, then put it down.

'There is something that perhaps you have not quite realized. As a sane man coming from another planet. Stevens is part of the Great Love Affair. He is the man who kept, or would have kept, the Blériots flying. As a man, they care for him nothing; as a part of their obsession, they care for him a lot. It is as in a love affair: when you love, you love passionately, jealously. So it is not just an engineer who has been taken away. It is a lover.'

He finished his coffee.

'Just warning you,' he said. 'That's all.'

When they got back to the workshop, they found the mechanics quietly working on the flying machines.

'That's right,' said Popadopoulos approvingly. 'After disaster has struck, the important thing is to get back to work.'

'Yes, well, but we don't know who we're working *for*.'

'I know who I'm working for,' said one of the mechanics. 'George's dad.'

'It's all right for you private people. But what about us?'

'You're all right, aren't you? The Government's buying three new Blériots and they'll still need you.'

'Yes, but who is going to be in charge of us? Now that Mr Stevens is gone, there's no one who knows anything about Blériots.'

'They'll appoint someone. Sure to.'

'Yes, well, I'm not so sure. Blériots cost money and they might change their mind.'

'It makes it more likely that they may want to call on the private machines.'

'Yes, but will they be keen on lending them? George's dad has gone off Blériots since he heard about the cables.'

'The best thing to do, lads, is just to keep on with what you were doing,' said Popadopoulos. 'Until someone tells you different.'

He went over to George's machine and peered into the cockpit.

'Anyone take the flask?' he asked. 'There was one. Mr Stevens fixed himself up with some coffee before they left.'

145

'It will be in there somewhere.'

'Well, it's not.'

'Are you sure?'

The mechanic went across and stuck his head into the cockpit.

'Well, I don't know where it's got to,' he said.

'They didn't pull it out with the – well, with Mr Stevens, did they?'

'If they did, it would have been on the ground some-where.'

'Unless those stretcher-bearers –'

'They wouldn't have taken it, would they?'

'Well, you never know with some of these people.'

'Maybe Maria picked it up?'

'Maria?' said Popadopoulos.

'My wife. She brings my lunch. And usually tidies up a bit while she's here.'

'And she –?'

'Over there. Back of the workshop.'

A woman was in the cubby-hole washing the mugs.

She showed one to Popadopoulos.

'Look at that!' she said. 'Filthy! I hope they don't keep their machines like that.'

'You're Maria, are you?'

'That's right.'

'Popadopoulos. Police.'

'Ah! The police, are you? I didn't think it would be long before you got here.'

'And you,' said Popadopoulos, 'are just the person I wanted to talk to!'

'Christ! Look, I don't know anything about it. I don't really belong around here –'

'That is just,' said Popadopoulos, 'why you are the per-son I need. Someone who stands outside it. Who can see things with an objective eye.'

'Really?'

146

He took her by the arm.

'Maria – if I can call you that?'

'You certainly can. As long as my husband isn't listening.'

'Maria, these men don't know how to look after themselves.'

'You can say that again!'

'They're all right on machines, but when it comes to basic things –'

'Well, some basic things they're very keen on.'

'Yes, I know. But I was thinking of food and drink. Cleaning up after themselves.'

'Never heard of it!'

'Mugs –'

'Disgusting!'

'It's just as well that you come in occasionally. Now, look, you're just the person who could tell me: what do they do when they want to make themselves a cup of coffee?'

'Well, it's not that difficult.'

'Mr Stevens, for instance? I gather he took a flask of coffee with him this morning when he went out with young Andreas.'

'Ah, well. Mr Stevens is a bit different. He's a bit picky about what he eats and drinks. A bit odd, too. But then, of course, he's an Englishman. I mean, our lads usually drink it black. A bit like lubricating oil, perhaps, but then, they probably feel more comfortable that way. But he didn't like it like that. He had to have milk in it. Always! And not any old milk. No! He said Greek milk was like goat's piss. Well, I'm just telling you, that's all. That's what he said. "It's the heat," I said. "It's the goats," he said. "Well, you can't do much about that," I said. "Can't you?" he said. "Can't you get any decent milk around here? Don't they have any cows?" "Well, of course they have cows," I said. "But they're up in the mountains." "Don't they ever come down here?" "No," I said.

'But then I thought. *They* don't come down here, but

147

there's a milkman who does. I've heard about him. He brings down milk for the Sultan, Or, at least, not for the Sultan. For the Sultan's –'

'Cat,' said Seymour.

'Well, yes, you're right,' she said, surprised. 'Who would have believed it? But the Sultan insists on it, apparently, so they have to go along with it, and they have to go to all the trouble of getting this bloke to come down from the mountains every day! It must cost them. I mean, you wouldn't do that for nothing. Come down all that way.

'But, anyway, I thought, if he's bringing some down for the Sultan, maybe he could spare some for Mr Stevens? Funnily enough, he wasn't keen. You would have thought he'd have been glad to make a bit extra, wouldn't you? But at first he even refused. "Look," I said, "it's for a big nob, an Englishman. He's famous all over Athens. He keeps those flying machines in the air." "I don't hold with those machines," he said. "If God had meant us to fly, he'd have given us wings." "We can use them against the Ottomans," I said. "At least, that's what my husband says." "Oh, can we?" he says. "Well, that's a bit different. Maybe I can spare a drop."

'So I fixed it up. He has to pass the base on his way to the Sultan's, so I got him to leave some each day. He used to put it just outside the door with a stone over the top so that nothing could get at it. And I would wash out the pot every day when I came round, because you can be sure those dirty sods would never think of doing that.'

Popadopoulos laughed.

'It's just as well they have you,' he said. 'Well, what a fuss over a lot of milk! But he was like that, you say?'

'Nico says he was just the same over the engines. Everything had to be just so.'

'And that, you reckon, was what he did this morning? When he was making himself the flask? Used the milk he'd had specially delivered?'

'Yes, because he was making it for himself. The others didn't like it like that. When the flask was for them they

148

would want it black. But he liked it almost all milk! So he used to make one for himself specially.'

'I was looking for the flask just now, but couldn't find it. You didn't pick it up, by any chance? To give it a wash?'

'No, it would have needed one before someone else used it. They're not exactly fussy but the taste can linger.'

'Well, there we are, Maria. Everyone likes his coffee the way he likes his coffee. I myself . . .'

Chapter Ten

'The milk?' said Seymour, as they walked away.

'It looks like it. He must have taken the poison this morning, either before or after taking off. We shall see what the laboratory has to say about the food he had for breakfast but I doubt if we shall find anything out of order there. He does not seem to have called in anywhere on his way to the workshop. So it looks as if he must have taken it there. Food? I did not see any. But liquid? That he certainly seems to have taken, certainly with him but possibly before.

'It was a pity that she washed up those mugs. We might have found traces. And a pity about the flask. We would perhaps have found traces there, too. I shall keep looking for the flask. I will ask the stretcher-bearers about it. But it may have fallen over the side of the cockpit, dropped, perhaps, as he leaned, or fell, back. It is possible he was trying to bring it to Mr Metaxas's attention, not suggesting he have a drink. He seemed very insistent.

'There are other things I need to know from the lab: what poison was it, how long would it take to work, what quantity would be necessary. Would the quantity he could have taken in that way be sufficient? He made his coffee with milk, but if it were the milk that was poisoned would that be enough?

'And then there are other questions, which perhaps I shall have to ask Mr Metaxas. He was there, apparently, all night. And then he went flying. Did he not have breakfast? Or at least some coffee? Which he might – would

150

naturally – have taken with Mr Stevens. A young man? Eat nothing? But perhaps he did take coffee, but not milk. That would be quite likely. I shall have to ask him. But yes, the milk.'

'I, too, have an interest in milk,' said Seymour. 'And, I suspect, the milkman.'

He told Popadopoulos about the cat.

Popadopoulos stopped.

'The cat, too? I had heard it had been poisoned but not of the milk. But that would not be surprising, would it? Milk, for a cat. And you say that it came from this man in the mountains?'

'Brought down especially.'

'And the same man, the same milk, perhaps, for Mr Stevens, too?'

'It looks like it.'

'I shall have to talk to that man.'

'You could talk to him tomorrow. When he next delivers the milk. Because he wouldn't know about Stevens. Or, at least, he shouldn't know. If he doesn't come, then –'

'Then I shall have some questions to ask him.'

'Do you mind if I am there too?'

'It would be a pleasure!' said Popadopoulos warmly. 'And, after all, does it not look as if the two things are connected?'

'It is odd,' said Popadopoulos a little later, as they were sitting at a table in Constitution Square, taking a pre-lunch ouzo together, 'that this cat should come back to haunt one. When the case came up, I could see it might come my way and I said, "No, thanks!" I didn't want to get involved in something so, well, foolish. But I need not have worried. They had decided not to put me on it already.'

He looked at Seymour and smiled.

'I have, you see, a past. What is worse in Athenian eyes, an Ottoman past. I am not, in fact, an Athenian. I grew up in Salonica and my mother is Turkish. That is not unusual in Salonica, the mixture, I mean. The whole city is like that. And it is, in fact, an Ottoman city. It is part of the Ottoman Empire and ruled by an Ottoman Governor.

'Well, that did not matter to me. There are plenty of Greeks in the city, and my father was Greek. I prefer the Greek way of doing things so I moved to Athens. But ever afterwards I have been slightly suspect in their eyes. Not a true Greek, they feel. I sometimes think that they believe my mother's blood is bound to come out at some time. And I have noticed that they do not assign me to cases where the two sides of me, as they believe, might come into conflict.

'As in the case of the Sultan. If it is true that the cat might be a sighting shot for the Sultan, then they don't want a possible Ottoman sympathizer getting mixed up in it. Particularly one who grew up in Salonica, because Salonica, you see, is where the Sultan was first sent to when he was exiled from Istanbul. It was part of the Ottoman Empire but a long way away. He would have few sympathizers there and the Ottoman police could keep an eye on him.

'But might I not be one of their agents? I had plenty of Ottoman contacts there after all. Who knows what secret instructions I may have received! Of course, it is a lot of nonsense. My inclinations have always been towards the Greeks and that is why I came to Athens.

'But I can understand their doubts, especially at the present time when there is every prospect of us going to war. And when the first target of the Greek army is likely to be Salonica!

'So I am slightly suspect. And I am suspect for another reason, too. I believe it is foolish to go to war. I have lived in a city where Greeks and Ottomans live side by side and get on well together. Why, now, do they have to fight each other? There is this crazy idea of Venizelos's that the Greeks all over the world ought to get together and form a Greater Greece! But what about me? Half of me says yes, I want to belong to Greece. But the other half says hey, wait a minute, I don't want to go to war about this, we can manage perfectly well without that. What's wrong with it as it is? A glorious fudge, yes, but what's wrong with a glorious fudge? Especially in the Balkans. It's the only thing that makes sense.

'And that is what I say to my bosses. "I am the only man who makes sense." "Oh, is that so, Popadopoulos?" they say. And they usually give me some shit job. "Well, you make sense of that!" And that is what I thought they had done now. An Englishman killed. That's bad. The English will be up your ass. Whose ass is it best for them to be up? Why, Popadopoulos's, of course!

'But now I find that perhaps there is a connection between this murdered Englishman and the Ottoman cat! They have not got me away from the Ottomans after all.

'Nor, it seems, after all, from the cat. "No, thanks!" I said. And when they said, "Christ, it's an Ottoman cat. We must keep Popadopoulos away!", I played along. "Oh, goodness!" I said. "It's an Ottoman cat! Am I reliable? Can you trust me?" Because I didn't want anything to do with something so damned foolish. And I thought I'd got away with it.'

He shook his head pretend-mournfully.

'But now it looks as if I haven't. Nor from the Ottomans, either. Oh, dear, I'm afraid it looks as if they'll have to put up with me.'

He slapped Seymour playfully on the arm and roared with laughter.

'You bring me luck, my friend. Because it looks as if whatever they do, they can't get away from me!'

He put down his glass.

'And now,' he said, 'I have to make some enquiries. I have to go back and see if all is as it seems. If, for instance, Mr Stevens really was as much of a family man as his landlady supposes. A man on his own, away from his wife? In Athens? I think it unlikely. Perhaps I shall have another word with Maria. And with the mechanics, too.

And visit the young men as well. Surely there must have been passions for things other than Blériots!'

At the hotel Seymour found waiting for him a note from the British Embassy. It asked him to call on the Ambassador that afternoon. When he did so, he found the Ambassador in a meeting.

'It's with the Greeks,' said Farquhar. 'They're very burned up about Stevens. They want to know what we are going to do about it.'

'What do they want you to do?'

'Raise it with the Ottomans. They're sure they're behind it.'

'And are you going to?'

'Not yet. The Old Man says you can't be sure that it is the Ottomans. He wants the case investigated first.'

'They're doing that. They've got a good man on the job.'

'Old Pop? He's a character, isn't he? I like him but for some reason the Greeks don't seem too sure of him.'

'Well, he's getting on with it.'

'Look, can you stay close to him? Obviously it's not up to you to conduct the investigation but the Old Man would like to be kept informed. It's a British national, after all. I think he'll be putting that point to them now and I expect they'll go along with it. And would you draft me a report? What happened, people involved, cause of death, that sort of thing. Implications for Anglo-Greek relations. Although perhaps I'd better handle that. Look, can you do it as a draft, and I'll tart it up as necessary. I'll mention that you are fortunately on the scene and are involving yourself in the case. They'll be pleased about that. Especially Scotland Yard. In a way it gives us more of an excuse to have you out here.'

Seymour settled down with pencil and paper. It didn't take him long. There wasn't much to say. But afterwards he thought, as he always did, that an existence had disappeared, forever, and that a gap was left.

When he had finished, he took the draft to Farquhar.

'Thanks, old man. And thanks for your help this morning. Oh, incidentally, I took young Metaxas back home afterwards. He was very shaken up and I had the carriage there. Handed him over to his mother. She sends you her greetings. The daughter was there, too. Stunning girl, isn't she?'

After leaving the Embassy, Seymour made his way to the ex-Sultan's residence, arriving there about teatime. He had found that a good time to talk to people there. They were just getting up from their siestas and beginning to pick up their tasks again. It was a particularly good time to catch the kitchen servants since they were all there and the evening meal still some time away.

He had hardly begun to talk to them, however, when Orhan Eser appeared.

'I was beginning to wonder where you were,' he said disapprovingly. Evidently he had now come to include Seymour in those people for whom he felt a responsibility and a need to keep on their toes.

'I had something to do for the Ambassador.'

'Oh, yes?'

'He wanted me to look into the murder of a British national.'

'Oh?' said Orhan Eser, indifferently.

'An engineer. He's been working on the flying machines.'

'The flying machines?'

'Yes. I know you've been taking an interest in them. I thought you might like to know.'

'Did you say he had been murdered?'

'I did. This morning.'

Orhan Eser seemed taken aback.

'The one who's opened a workshop on the army base?'

'Yes.'

'Really? Murdered?'

'Yes.'

Orhan Eser shook his head.

'That is unfortunate,' he said.

'Sad for his family.'

'And for the Greeks, too,' said Orhan Eser. With a bitter flash of something that may have been humour.

That will be some information that will soon be on its way to Istanbul, thought Seymour.

He saw a bent black form slip out of the kitchen and followed it along the corridor until it came to the dark space underneath the stairs where they kept brooms and brushes and cleaning materials. There it settled down.

'Hello, Amina!' said Seymour. 'That's your comfy place, is it?'

Amina looked up at him suspiciously.

'I've got a right to a place to sit down, haven't I? A place of my own? At my age.'

'How old are you, Amina?'

'A hundred.'

'You don't look it. Fifty, I would say.'

Amina cackled.

'I passed fifty in the days of the old Sultan. No, the one before!'

'You've seen a lot in your time, Amina.'

'I have; and not much of it good, either.'

'What's it like here in Athens?'

'Filthy pigs!' she said vehemently.

'You preferred it back in Salonica?'

'I preferred it back in Istanbul, where people knew their place and the Sultan was properly respected.'

'He's come down in the world, hasn't he?'

'Yes, and some people have come up,' she said, with a meaningful glance back along the corridor to where he

156

could just see Orhan Eser standing talking to the senior kitchen servant.

'Was he with you in the palace?'

'In the palace? Him?' she said with scorn. 'They'd never have had him in the palace. He was doing the accounts in the barracks!'

'There was a step up for him, was there, when the officers took over?'

'There's always a need for people like him when there's a change. Someone who can tie things together while the ones at the top are getting on with more important things. There are new ladders and he thought he'd got his foot on one of them. He didn't like it a bit when they pulled him out and said they wanted him to go with the Sultan. "I'm too valuable here," he said. "You'll miss me." "You'll come back," they said. "We won't forget you. But meanwhile there's something important you have to do." So he went, but ever since then he's been hoping that they would call him back.'

'I expect there are quite a few people here who feel like that,' said Seymour.

'Oh, yes. Everyone wants to leave the setting sun.'

Along the corridor a door opened and Chloe came out carrying a great pile of plates.

'Of course, they wouldn't all want to go back to Istanbul,' said Seymour. 'I mean, there are some who come from round here.'

'We wouldn't have them if they did. They're unclean, idle. You can't train them. They answer back. I've had to go younger and younger. There was a day when a girl would have been proud to work in the Sultan's kitchen but they're not like that these days. Especially here. The Greeks! They would have been glad, too. It was like that when I started. We had lots of Greek women. But then they all fell away. When the Ottomans left. And now I can't get anyone. We have to go up into the mountains even to get baggages like that,' she said, nodding towards the struggling Chloe. 'The only thing they're good for is working on their back.'

She gave another loud cackle.

'And, of course, that's what they were used for. In the old days the Sultan's men would go round to all the villages looking for likely women and the men up there were only too willing to let them have them. They would be brought to the palace all weeping and wailing. "Listen, you silly bitches," I would say, "you've got it made! Play your cards right and you can go right to the top."

'And they could. "How do you think the senior wife got there? By playing her cards right. And now she runs the place! Not just the harem, you silly bitches. That's not what it's all about. But the palace, the Empire! Would you have had a chance of doing that if you hadn't been brought here? So shut up and get on with it."

'But, of course, it's not like that nowadays. The senior wife would be turning in her grave if she could see it now. The harem's nothing now. Just a few of his favourites. There isn't even a senior wife. I keep telling Abd-es-Salaam that he ought to get the Sultan to name one. Otherwise it's all squabbling and arguing. But he says, what's the point? It doesn't lead to anything. In the old days the senior wife ran the roost, but these days there isn't even a roost. I think he's just waiting for the Sultan to die. I think they're all waiting for the Sultan to die.'

Seymour went along to the kitchens. Orhan Eser wasn't there now and the servants were beginning to busy themselves with preparations for the evening meal. The senior servant, who didn't seem to have much to do at this point, saw him and came across to him.

'Hello, Effendi! We've just been having a cup of tea. Would you like some?'

'I would, indeed.'

'A chair for the Effendi!'

'No, no, don't bother.'

But a chair was brought, and later a cup of black tea. They had all got to know him now and seemed glad to see him. It was something different in their lives, he supposed. He wondered if Orhan Eser or Abd-es-Salaam ever sat down to take a cup of tea with them. He fancied not. The Ottoman Empire was in its way as hierarchical as the British one.

'So, Effendi,' said the senior servant, 'have you found out who killed the cat?'

'I will tell you an English nursery rhyme. It's called "Who Killed Cock Robin?"'

Everyone in the kitchen listened intently.

'Very good,' said the senior servant at the end. 'We've got one like that too. It's called "Who Killed Ali's Duck?"' He recounted it to Seymour. It had a chorus in which everyone in the kitchen joined in.

Seymour applauded.

'It's like that with the cat,' he said. 'A lot of people are involved but no one seems to have actually done the poisoning.'

'I myself think . . .' said the senior servant.

'Whereas I think . . .'

Everyone in the kitchen thought, not always, or, indeed, ever, helpfully. Seymour listened good-naturedly. At the end he said, straight-faced: 'The kitchen is a well of ideas. Put in a bucket and –'

'– you fetch up a load of rubbish,' someone finished.

There was a roar of laughter. Seymour got up from the chair.

'So I'm still looking. However, one thing, I imagine, that I don't need to look at these days is the quality of the milk. The herdsman no longer comes, I suppose?'

'That is true, Effendi.'

'I quite miss him, you know,' someone said. 'He was a sour old bugger but I quite liked him.'

'He still drops in occasionally,' said someone else, 'to see his niece.'

159

'Little Chloe?'

'Yes, I think he wants to be sure that she's getting on all right.'

'Which you can understand, since she's on her own here, and with that Amina on her back all the time.'

As he was leaving the kitchen Talal, the eunuch, came up to him.

'The Lady Samira would like to see you,' he said, 'on a matter of urgency.'

Seymour went with him obediently to the room in which he'd talked to Samira before. It was an inner room and there were no windows. The only light came from two oil lamps which were set back so that they would not throw any indecent light on a royal lady's face. There were two doors, the one through which he entered and another on the far side of the room, through which, shortly afterwards, Talal brought the dark, shapeless form of the Lady Samira.

Or was it shapeless? Despite the darkness, despite the muffling clothes and the long black veil, Seymour was able to make out a slim, elegant form. The all-encompassing robe, which at first he had taken for a normal *burka*, turned out to be a gown slit up the front and beneath it he could detect what looked distinctly like a stylish Parisian dress: and the veil, which began by being decently held up to and over Samira's nose, somehow slipped down more and more during the interview.

Without waiting for the eunuch to open proceedings, Samira launched at once into an attack.

'So,' she said to Seymour, in French, 'you dare to show your face?'

'I'm sorry?'

'After what you have done!'

'After what I have done?' asked the bewildered Seymour, looking at Talal for enlightenment. The eunuch gave a baffled shrug. 'What have I done?'

160

'Don't pretend you don't know. The eunuchs tell me you ordered it. Isn't that so, Talal?'

'I haven't told you anything!' cried Talal.

'But what –'

'The medicine! You pried into my medicine. Has a woman no privacy? Has a man no decency?'

'I am very sorry if I have offended you. It was part of a general enquiry, that's all. I merely wished to find out what substances might have come into the harem. There was nothing personal –'

'You pry into my more intimate details and then you say there was nothing personal?'

'Lady Samira, as far as I can recall, in your case it was only aspirins –'

'But it could have been something much more – more *intimate*. Mr Seymour, I am shocked at this invasion of my privacy. And shocked that you, who appeared to be such a sensitive, understanding man –'

'Look, I'm very sorry, but –'

'And then you say there was nothing personal! I could have forgiven it – almost – if there was. If, say, I felt that you had been driven to penetrate to my innermost core –'

'Lady Samira, this is bordering on the indecent!'

'Shut up, Talal. But you tell me there was nothing personal. I am hurt, Mr Seymour. Hurt! It is so cold of you. I almost wish there *had* been something personal. Well, I would have been shocked, of course, but I would have understood it, and perhaps even forgiven it. But what I cannot forgive is this cold prying.'

'Lady Samira, I assure you that nothing could have been further from my intentions.'

'Really?'

'Well, yes. That is –'

'I suppose I could forgive you,' said Lady Samira thoughtfully. 'You have a job to do, I understand that. And I *did* say I would help you. You want to know how the poison got into the harem. And you thought it might come

161

in in the guise of medicine. But, you know, other things come in too. The sort of stuff that Talal gets in, for instance.'

'What!' said Talal, startled.

'The stuff for your hair, I mean. To make it grow again.'

'This is not true,' said Talal stiffly.

'And the other stuff. To restore – well, you know, restore you to what you were. But it won't work, Talal. They've cut them off.'

'This is all completely untrue,' Talal said to Seymour.

'We all have our secrets. Irina, for instance. She gets in love potions.'

'Who for?' said Talal sceptically.

'The Sultan, of course. Well, poor dear, she needs them. If she's going to get anywhere. Of course, the rest of us can manage without.'

Seymour laughed.

'I think you're the tiniest bit malicious, Lady Samira. Actually, I know the kind of medicine that the Lady Irina has been taking, and she's been putting it to a rather different use than you suppose.'

'Has she? Well, I don't know anything about that. I was talking about love potions. Well, Mr Seymour, we must end our conversation. This kind of talk makes Talal over-excited. We must continue on another occasion. I said I would help you and I think I can.'

'You already have,' said Seymour.

He was meeting Aphrodite. By the time he got to Constitution Square it was getting dark and waiters were going round lighting the candles on the tables. But over to the west the sun had not yet completely set and the sky was still red and bronze. The combination, the soft darkness close at hand and the rapidly disappearing brightness far off, was magical. Nothing like this in the East End. In fact, you weren't conscious of sky at all in the East End.

162

Aphrodite was sitting at a table waiting for him. She seemed tense.

'What's the matter?' he said.

She shrugged.

'Oh, nothing.'

Then she said: 'A detective has been at our house all afternoon.'

'Yes, I know. Mr Popadopoulos. He said he might be going to see you.'

'You know him?'

'Well, I've met him. What are you worried about? He's all right.'

'Yes, he's perfectly polite. But why is he spending so much time with us?'

'I don't think he is. He's spending time with everybody.'

'It's making my mother very unhappy. I don't think I've ever seen her so agitated. She thinks Andreas is in trouble.'

'No, he's not. It's just that he happened to be there and Popadopoulos wants to know all he can about it.'

'He keeps going on about some flask.'

'We think it may have been a drink from that that poisoned Stevens.'

'Why don't they just analyse it?'

'Because they can't find it. At least, they couldn't while I was there. It may have fallen over the side. You know, in flight.'

'He keeps asking Andreas about it.'

'Well, it's important.'

'And Andreas doesn't know. It looks bad. He says he can't remember.'

'Well, he probably can't. He remembers Stevens poking him with it and thought it was just that he wanted him to have a drink. I suspect he was trying to tell Andreas that there was something wrong with it.'

Aphrodite was hardly listening.

'And then he switched. Popadopoulos, I mean. He

163

started asking questions about what had happened earlier. Before the flight. When Stevens had got there. What did they do? Did they have breakfast? Breakfast! Well, I ask you! Of course, I realize that at some point Stevens took poison and that it could have been then. But . . .

'He made it sound so *suspicious*. My father says that's because it *is* suspicious. Andreas was the only other person there. If someone gave him the poison, then it has to be Andreas.

'Of course, my mother hit the roof. She was beside herself. She said how could he suppose, even suppose, such a thing? He said of course he didn't suppose it. Not for one moment. But this was the way it could look. Well, you can just imagine what it's like in our house tonight! Somehow we seem to have been dragged into this stupid, horrible thing.'

Chapter Eleven

When Seymour left the hotel it was the middle of the night. Life went on late in Athens but now the streets were dark and deserted. A thin wind was stirring the dust and as he approached the army base it developed an edge. The dust now was blowing strongly into his face, the small particles cutting his skin. Without the sun Athens seemed suddenly a bleak, cold place.

The base was still and empty and Stevens' workshop, now without the flying machines – they were back in their original workshops on the other side of the aerodrome – seemed oddly derelict. He tried the door. It opened, and as he went in a hand touched his arm. Popadopoulos was already there.

They settled down to wait without speaking. Both of them had done this kind of thing before.

Seymour half expected the herdsman not to show up. Had it not been a special thing, his coming down from the mountains to the Sultan's house? Arranged especially by the Acting-Vizier? And yet somehow Maria had worked Stevens in on the act. But had the act continued after the cat had gone? Oddly, it seemed to have.

Either his eyes were getting used to the dark or it was getting lighter. It was getting lighter. Popadopoulos opened the door a fraction. He could see now, just outside the door, the pot put there for the milk, with the flat stone lying on top of it. Popadopoulos had obviously arranged for it to be put out as usual. Perhaps he had even put it there himself.

Then, suddenly, he heard the clip-clopping of hooves. The hooves came up to the workshop and stopped. There was movement just outside the door.

Popadopoulos stepped out.

There was a startled exclamation.

'It's all right!' said the detective soothingly. 'It's just the police.'

'What the hell's going on?' said the herdsman.

'Popadopoulos. And you must be Ari.'

Seymour came out too.

'Christ, another one! Are you really the police? Look, if you want trouble –'

'We are really the police,' said Popadopoulos, 'and we'd like a word with you.'

'Why do you have to come upon me like that?'

'How else are we to come upon you? You're never here in respectable hours.'

'I've got to get back to my cows.'

'Of course. And you'll be able to very shortly. But first some questions.'

'I've seen you before,' said Ari, looking at Seymour.

'Yes, you have. In the Sultan's house. I was interested in the cat, remember?'

'What happened to the cat is nothing to do with me. I bring good milk. If someone in the Sultan's house has added something to it, that's their concern, not mine.'

'They don't need your milk at the Sultan's house now,' said Seymour. 'The cat's dead. How is it you're still coming down?'

'I deliver it to Spiro's too. Well, since I was coming down . . .'

'Who is Spiro?' asked Seymour.

'He has a shop in the Plaka, a posh shop. Not big, but posh for posh people. And apparently they like milk. Not milk so much as cream. They're willing to pay over the odds for it, so I thought, why not? Of course, Spiro makes something out of it. In fact, Spiro makes a *lot* out of it. More than I do. But that's the way it is, isn't it? It's the

166

middleman who makes the money, not the poor sod who produces it. Not that I've got anything against Spiro. He's married Eleni, from our village. And he seems to have treated her all right. I reckon it was Eleni who suggested it to him. The cream, I mean. When she knew I was coming down to the Sultan.'

'And it's worth your while carrying on, then?' said Popadopoulos. 'Even without the Sultan?'

'Just about.'

'And even dropping some in here?'

'Ah, well, that was just doing someone a favour. I don't really do individuals. But this lady asked. She'd heard about me from Eleni. And apparently there's this bloke, he's an Englishman – you wouldn't think, would you, that an Englishman would know about milk, but it seems –'

'Not any longer,' said Popadopoulos. 'The Englishman's dead.'

'Dead! But – here, what's going on? Why are you asking me these questions? What did he die of?'

'Poison.'

'You're not suggesting . . . Listen, someone's got something against me. First the cat and then . . . It's envy, that's what it is. They see me doing all right and they think, Christ, I'll have a bit of that. They think that just because we're different from them then we're not entitled to a living the same as they are. As soon as a Vlach starts doing well, there's always someone who wants to stop it. Greek, Ottoman, they're all the same. Always looking out for a chance to jump on us! But if anyone thinks they're going to put one across on me –'

'All right, all right,' said Popadopoulos soothingly. 'No one's trying to put something across on you. We are just interested, that's all. And I'm especially interested. Look, if the Sultan wanted your milk, that says something, doesn't it? It must be good. And if Spiro's in on it too . . . Listen, I know Spiro and he's no fool. There must be something special about your milk. You know, I'd like to try it. Here, let me have a sip. Just a sip. There could be something for you in this. I know someone –'

The herdsman was persuaded.

'Delicious!' said Popadopoulos, smacking his lips. 'That milk is something! How about a sip for my friend, too? He's English and he knows something about milk. There are a lot of cows in England, and grass, too.'

'Ah, but are there mountains? Spring pastures? Spring pastures give a special taste.'

'Well, that's true, Ari. I'm prepared to tell anyone that your milk is special. Really something! So if there are any questions about it, it will be because something has been put in.'

'Well, you're right about that. And that's what I said to Orhan Eser. "Are you complaining?" I said. "No," he said. "Just wondering, that's all. The cat –" "If anyone's been putting something into the cat's milk," I said, "it's one of your lot. Not me. It's fresh from the cow and I'm with it the whole time until it gets here. So it's *after* I get here. One of that lot in the kitchen, I reckon. Or maybe one of the crazy bitches in the harem. That's more like. You want to be looking at them, not me." "Well, maybe I do," said Orhan Eser. "And maybe I will."

'I quite get on with him, you know. A lot of people don't. He's always on to them, they say. Well, I think someone *should* be on to them, because, from what I've seen, they don't do an honest day's work between them.

'And he was fair about stopping the milk. "Here's payment for two extra weeks," he said. "I know it's hard up in the mountains. I've been up in the mountains myself." I was a bit surprised at that, you know, but maybe that explains it. Why he's got a bit of time for me. Because he has, I think; I don't think he's putting it on.

'I was in there the other day, to ask after my niece, little Chloe, you know, and he saw me in the kitchen and he said, "What are you doing here, Ari?" Because he thought, you see, that I was trying to get them to take more milk. "We don't need it now, Ari," he said, a bit sharply.

168

'So I explained I was just there to see little Chloe, and that I had other customers in the city now. I told him about Spiro and about here, and about another place I've got my eye on, and he changed his tune. "You've been doing well, Ari," he says. "And you're coming down every day? That's good. It will build up, you know. Anyway, good luck to you, and don't worry about Chloe, I'll keep my eye on her and see that Amina doesn't bear too hard on her." That's what he said, and I thought it was handsome of him. You know, with a name for being high-and-mighty. But I speak as I find, and I've always found him all right.'

'You still meet these people from time to time,' said Pop-adopoulos after he had gone. 'The old sort. But you don't find them in the city so much nowadays. You find them in villages in the country, or maybe up in the mountains, where he comes from. He's a Vlach.'

'Yes, so I gather. They've got a bit of a name for being independent-minded, so I'm told.'

'Yes. Some people find them truculent but I don't. More independent-minded, as you said. And able. You find them in all sorts of places nowadays. My boss is a Vlach.'

'What I don't understand,' said Seymour, 'is what Orhan Eser was doing up in the mountains. He's not a Vlach, is he?'

'He's a Turk. With a name like that. And it is surprising, yes. The Ottomans don't have a good name with the Vlachs, and they usually keep out of the mountains. A soldier, perhaps?'

The wind had increased in strength and the dust particles were now a blizzard. The few people who were around walked with their faces covered. Looking down, Seymour saw that his clothes were white with dust.

'If it was the milk,' said Seymour, 'someone must have put it in after it was delivered.'

'Someone at the base, that looks like,' said Pop-adopoulos. 'And that fits with the cables. I shall have to go back there.'

Seymour, meanwhile, was thinking about Vlachs. He went back to the Sultan's house and looked for Chloe.

'I met your uncle,' he said.

'Did you?' said Chloe, brightening.

'Yes. He said he'd been dropping in to see you.'

'Well, he has. And that's funny, because he never took much notice of me back up in the village. I daresay people have been on to him. Although the truth is, he doesn't take much notice of *anybody.*'

'Vlachs are like that, I gather,'said Seymour. He looked at her. 'You're a Vlach yourself, of course, aren't you, Chloe?'

'I am.'

'And – wait a minute – didn't someone tell me that Lady Irina was a Vlach, too?'

'She is.'

'Did you all know each other, up in the mountains?'

'Oh, no!' Chloe chuckled. 'The Lady Irina is *much* older than me. And she comes from another part of the mountains. And that was a long, long time ago. But she was in a village like mine. She told me about it once.'

'And then the Sultan's men came and took her away?'

'The soldiers came.'

'Did they come to your village too?'

'No. We were lucky. But they went to a lot of villages. And did terrible things and afterwards everyone was very hungry. The Lady Irina told me. She said that people were so poor that they sometimes had to sell their children. That's what happened to her, she said. She didn't much mind at the time, she said, because everything was so horrible. Even in the harem it was better. But it got worse later on. She said I mustn't stay here, no matter what my family say. And she spoke to my uncle about it.'

170

'She spoke to your uncle? How did she manage that?'

'Ah, well,' said Chloe, and scuttled away.

Seymour had been aware, all the time that he was talking to Chloe, of Talal lurking up the corridor. Now he came forward.

'Effendi,' he said, plucking Seymour's arm, 'a word with you.'

'Of course.'

'Effendi, it is not true!' the eunuch said urgently. 'What she said.'

'She?'

'The Lady Samira. It is not true. I do not take anything to restore my hair. Nor my – nor to overcome what has been done.'

'I didn't suppose it was true, Talal.'

'Thank you, Effendi. That woman: she is indecent, malicious. She likes to strike at people. She was always like that. But it has been worse, much worse, since we left Istanbul. In the old harem, Effendi, she was a nobody. She did not bear a child. So we were all surprised when His Highness chose her to come to Salonica. Some said she must have practised some black art upon him. Or given him some drug. For otherwise why should he choose her?

'But I will tell you, Effendi. She is a scheming woman. And somehow she made him. Whether it was an art she had learnt in her village or whether it was her woman's wiles, I do not know. But somehow she got herself on to the party that left for Salonica.

'It was a small party, Effendi, compared with what we had been used to. In the old harem there had been dozens; in the new, less than one. And in this she saw her chance. The Sultan had not appointed a new senior wife and she meant to be the one he chose.

'Daily – or, rather, nightly – she badgers him. Still he refuses: but for how long, Effendi? Will he not become

171

weary and give in to her importunities? That is what we fear. And we whisper in Abd-es-Salaam's ear. We say that it is not right that a woman who cannot bear a child should aspire to be senior wife. It is a breach with all tradition. It makes a mockery of the title.

'But Abd-es-Salaam tells us that was part of the deal. That he could live out his life but that there were to be no children. And perhaps that is so, for the Lady Irina is another such as the Lady Samira.

'We would prefer the Lady Irina, although she is not a woman but a tiger. But we do not think that the Lady Irina wishes to be the senior royal wife. She just doesn't want the Lady Samira to be it. And so they fight for supremacy, Effendi, and who knows who will win?

'For, Effendi, they scheme and they plot and they contrive. They wrestle all the time. And since our move to Athens it has become worse. Because they both see it as an opportunity: Samira, as an opportunity to become first wife; Irina as an opportunity to – I know not what, but there is a new light in her eyes, and we fear, we fear . . .

'The death of the cat made us tremble. For if the cat, why not the Sultan? Maybe Irina wishes to break free and makes an essay upon the cat to see if it can be done. Or maybe it is different – if that is what she has in mind, would she draw attention to it by first striking at the cat in such a way? Perhaps it is the Lady Samira who poisons the cat so that it would seem as if that was what the Lady Irina had in mind, so that then she might free herself of her rival and step unchallenged into the place she seeks.'

'My mother is a Vlach,' said Aphrodite.

The point had come up because he had been telling her about Chloe.

'So she is. I remember you telling me. But that means you're one, too.'

'Half one. It doesn't feel any different.'

'Do you think it feels different for her?'

'She doesn't talk much about it. I think she thinks of herself as Greek.'

'Does she have many Vlach friends?'

'I don't think so. Not particularly. She goes to Vlach shops when she can. I think she likes to give them business.'

'Spiro's?'

'Sometimes. It's a good shop. But Spiro's not a Vlach. His wife is, but he's not. You know Spiro's?'

'No. I've just heard the name. But the person who mentioned it was a Vlach and I wondered if they tended to stick together.'

'I don't know that they do especially,' said Aphrodite doubtfully. 'Why are you asking?'

'I was wondering if they supported each other. I was thinking of Chloe. She needs to get away from the harem. Find someone else she can work for.'

'I'll mention it around.'

They went on to have dinner and study the moonlight over the Parthenon and such things.

The next morning, though, he was at the workshop bright and early.

'Hello!' they said. 'You again?'

'I'm just checking on one or two things. For a report I've got to write. It's for the people back in London.'

'Check away, then.'

Seymour walked over to the flying machines. There were only two of them this morning.

'Is the other one already out?'

'No, no, no. It's over there.'

They pointed to the other side of the runway.

'It's gone back home. To where they used to keep it.'

Seymour looked at the machines.

'You know,' he said, 'I can't tell the difference between them. Which one is the one that Mr Stevens was out in?'

'This one. It's George's, but he lets Andreas fly it. And Mr Stevens, of course.'

'Did Mr Stevens often fly them?'

'No. He could fly – he'd got his licence. But he said he got his kicks from getting them up there, not from being up there. I'm like that myself. And Maria tells me it had better stay that way. We're expecting a baby and now is not the time, she says, for me to be doing silly things. Like flying over mountains or fighting in silly wars.'

'Well, she's got a point, you know.'

'She has. But there's more to it than she thinks. There are not many jobs like this around. How many Blériot machines does Athens need? Six? Five? And if one of them crashes, only four. And if two of them crash – well, it's back on the motor cars for me. War would actually help, if it makes them get more machines. Though I don't say this to her.'

'She'll be coming in, will she, a bit later?'

'As usual. With my lunch.'

'She'll have to make a decision about the milk. Will you want it now that Stevens is not here?'

'Not as far as I'm concerned. What's wrong with goat's milk? I don't go for all this fancy stuff.'

'She was very clever to have found a way of getting it for him,' said Seymour. 'How did she come upon that old herdsman? You wouldn't exactly run into him on the street, would you? Not at four o'clock in the morning.'

'Someone put her on to him. A shop she goes to.'

'Not Spiro's, was it?'

'It could have been.'

'Hey, she's not a Vlach, is she?'

'Vlach? You must be joking! She's as Greek as moussaka. Comes from Salonica.'

'Salonica's not Greece,' objected one of the mechanics.

'It is as far as she is concerned. And Venizelos, too. Otherwise why are we fighting this bloody war?'

The soldiers still hadn't moved. Or, rather, according to Dr Metaxas, they had moved. They had gone out and then came back again, and now they were camped in a vineyard about halfway between Athens and the mountains, where they were testing the local product to see that it had not fallen off.

Seymour had seen Dr Metaxas as he was crossing the square. He was sitting alone at a table, his drink before him. He looked up as Seymour approached.

'Hello!' he said. 'Are you looking for my Nemesis? She's not here yet.'

Seymour felt a twinge of discomfort at this reference to Aphrodite. It seemed to take for granted that there was a relationship between them. Well, of course there was. But how far did their assumption go?

He suddenly remembered again what Old Tsakatellis had said, back in London. 'Greek women,' he had said, 'are *different*. You don't treat them as you do these trollops around here. You treat them with respect!'

Well, that was all right. He had every intention of treating Aphrodite with respect and thought he had done so. But that, he knew deep down, was not quite what Tsakatellis had meant. He had meant that the moment you started going out with a Greek girl, a thicket of family expectations suddenly sprang up around you.

'What you've got to remember,' Old Tsakatellis had said, 'is that with a Greek girl, it's not just her you're going out with, it's the whole family.'

He knew what that meant. It was not so very different in the conservative, traditional East End where many of the immigrant families had brought their traditions with them. Go out with an unmarried girl once, and suddenly every-one in the street had an eye on you. Go out twice and the family started getting ideas. Go out three times and that

175

meant either that an understanding had been reached or that the girl was, in East End terms, a trollop.

Was it the same here? He suspected that it was. The thought of Andreas hanging around the table that evening, obviously uncomfortable at seeing his sister sitting alone with a man, suddenly came back to him.

But, hang on a moment. Aphrodite herself had clearly not felt uncomfortable. In fact, she had felt irritated at being dragged away. But, of course, she would, and that didn't mean that was how the family would see it. Aphrodite was an unusually independent woman, not just for a Greek woman but for any woman. A New Woman, he had thought her. And so she was, going to university, studying to become a doctor and all that.

But was she as New as this? He had an uneasy feeling that when the chips were down she might take to seeing things as an Old Woman would, and an Old Greek Woman at that!

Come, come, now, he told himself. He was making too much of this. Things were hardly at that point yet. A warm friendship, that's all it was. Aphrodite was a modern girl and she would certainly see it like that.

But would her family? Would she be able to hold out against her whole family? She was unusually independent, yes, but would she be able to manage that?

Seymour knew something about this. He came from immigrant stock himself. He knew about family pressure. That time when he had told them he was going into the police! And about every time he stopped to talk to a girl. The whole street, the whole neighbourhood, reported back and his mother started getting into conversations. It was the same with his sister. A real dog-fight that had turned into! About every week his mother enquired 'how things were going'. 'Marvellously,' his sister replied. 'And I'm *not* getting married!' Oh yes, Seymour knew all about family pressure!

But, come, he was making too much of this. His mind was getting as lurid as his mother's. All that had happened was that he had been out with Aphrodite once or twice. And that first time, the Melaxases had even suggested it!

But what about last night? And that other time they had had dinner together? And . . .?

He had taken her home afterwards and they hadn't seemed to mind. Aphrodite certainly hadn't minded.

Well, no, but where exactly did Aphrodite stand on this? He had assumed she felt exactly as he did. But wasn't he taking too much for granted? Suppose . . .

And how did he feel, anyway? Deep down?

Well, he knew that, at any rate. It was all too early. That was the trouble with families. They jumped to conclusions, put pressure on you prematurely. You had to stave them off. That was what families were all about, finding space for yourself, staving them off.

Too early. He was sure Aphrodite would feel the same.

But he knew that wasn't it. The question was how her family felt. And might he not have let things go a little too far?

And there was her father, sitting benignly opposite him, sipping his ouzo and looking at him!

Her father: he clutched at that. He was a reasonable man, modern, free-thinking if anything, against monarchism and such, with, surely, a very liberal attitude towards his daughter, wanting her to go to university, to become a doctor.

But that remark of his, which had started this whole train of thought off, that taking for granted that there *was* a relationship, that assumption that Seymour might know more about his daughter's plans than he did – was he reading too much into this, or was it a hint?

Seymour decided to take the bull by the horns.

'I hope you don't think, Dr Metaxas, that I'm seeing too much of your daughter?'

Dr Metaxas waved a hand.

'Aphrodite does what she wants.' He sighed. 'Always has.'

'I am aware that, coming from England, my ways may not be Greek ways.'

Dr Metaxas waved again: a slight dismissive gesture.

'She probably thinks that an advantage.'

'The trouble is that there is also the question of how others see them.'

'Well . . .' said Dr Metaxas indulgently.

'Andreas, I think, is not altogether comfortable.'

'Andreas is a blockhead.'

Dr Metaxas finished his glass and looked around for the waiter. This time it was Seymour who signalled.

'Aphrodite will go her own way. Never mind what I think or say or do. I have always encouraged that. But . . .'

'But?'

Dr Metaxas sipped his new ouzo.

'But her mother may not be of the same mind.'

He examined his glass.

'That will be something to look forward to,' he said: 'Aphrodite versus her mother. At least it will make a change from Aphrodite versus me. I await the result with interest.'

'These are difficult times for my family,' he suddenly said. 'For my wife especially.'

'Of course.'

'Popadopoulos was over, asking questions. She didn't like that. "It's his job," I said. "He doesn't mean anything by it." But the drift of his questions was obvious. Someone put poison in Stevens' flask that morning and the only other person over there was Andreas. I told him that Andreas was the last person who would poison Stevens. He idolized him. Ridiculously. Not only that; he relied on him. He needed his help to go on flying, and that was what he cared about most in the world. Yes, yes, yes, he said: but I knew what he was thinking.

'She could see it, too, and it drove her almost mad with anxiety. She cares for him desperately. Well, every mother does. But perhaps she is over-protective. She had got herself into a state over his flying, anyway, and then the war came along and made it worse.' He looked at Seymour. 'You can have no idea of the effect it had on her.'

'Perhaps I do,' said Seymour, 'a little. Stevens told me about her experiences in the mountains. She's a Vlach, isn't she?'

'*Stevens* told you?' said Dr Metaxas, surprised.

'Yes. He'd had it from Andreas.'

Dr Metaxas shrugged. 'She detested Stevens. She thought he was leading Andreas astray.'

'To do him justice,' said Seymour, 'he understood that. He told me he was determined to see that Andreas came to no harm. He said he would see that he never got across the mountains. I have a hunch that that may have been why he was with him that day – to make sure he stayed this side of the mountains.'

'Really?' said Dr Metaxas. 'Perhaps I will tell her that when she's calmer.'

'He asked me to tell her.'

'I *will* tell her that. Perhaps it will make her think more kindly of him.'

He shrugged. 'Not that it matters now.'

He emptied his glass.

'Did you know that I was up in the mountains myself during the war?' he said. 'The last war. Her war.'

'Stevens did mention it.'

'I met Orhan Eser up there. I had a shock when they called me in to see the Sultan and I found him. I recognized him at once. Of course, he was much younger then. Barely a boy. He was in charge of transport on their side and for a while we had to work together.

'There had been an engagement. Many wounded. We arranged a time so that we could evacuate them. It took

179

some time because it snowed and the roads were blocked. So I got to know him quite well. We had a lot of talks together. Got on well. We were very alike in some respects. He was all for modernizing, reforming, improving, and so – in those days – was I. I realize now that he was one of what we would call now the Young Turks. That's why I was surprised to see him there at the Sultan's. I found him very reasonable, I must say.

'He helped me get her down. When I ran into him at the Sultan's, I reminded him about it and said that it had ended up with me marrying her. He seemed very moved and said that it showed there was a God after all.

'I was going to tell her about it but then I thought I wouldn't. The memories are still too painful, you know. It's all still with her. The war has brought it back. I think that's maybe why she feels so strongly about Andreas – and about Popadopoulos's questions.'

'I wouldn't worry about Andreas if I were you.'

'Oh, I'm not,' said Dr Metaxas. 'It's her I'm worried about.'

Chapter Twelve

'Feel like a drink, old man? Before lunch?' said Farquhar. 'I do. I've been writing to the family. I know it's only a draft and it will come as from the Old Man. But he only signs it. I do the writing; and it's not much fun when it's something like this.'

'You've been writing about Stevens?'

'To the family, yes. I must say, seeing that photograph in his lodgings brought it home to me. Wife, kids. You wonder about the set-up. Who will look after them? Is there any money? He was out here on a contract: will the Greek Government do anything for them? He had only been here a short time, and the Government doesn't have money to spare. Of course, I don't ask about these things in the letter, but you can't help wondering. What'll it be, old man? Beer, whisky, sherry? I'm going for a whisky myself this morning. We've got some good malts here.'

He led Seymour into the small bar.

'What with one thing and another, it's all pretty depressing,' he said. 'Stevens, the war.'

'Has it actually started?'

'Getting pretty close. We thought we could stave it off. Keep this business about the Sultan going. Everyone seemed to be playing along and we thought that was what they all wanted. Deep down, you know. I mean, war's a serious thing and we thought they won't really want it, they're just playing games. That's what they do in the Balkans. But then it suddenly blows up and becomes real.

181

And that's the Balkans, too. You think it's all hunky-dory and then suddenly it isn't.'

'They're not bothered about the Sultan any longer?'

'They've decided they don't need an excuse.'

'So they're not bothered about the cat, either?'

'Well, I don't think they were ever exactly *bothered* about the cat. It was just part of the game.'

'So I can go home?'

'Just wrap it up decently, old man, so that we can put it to bed.'

'Do you still want to know who did it?'

'Depends who did it, old man.'

'Someone in the harem.'

'An inside job, as you chaps say? Splendid! Not the Greeks? Or the Ottomans? Or anyone else? Well, that *is* good news. Not a political job after all. I'll tell the Old Man. He *will* be pleased.'

'I can say who did it?'

'Publish it far and wide, old man. If it's someone in the harem. It doesn't matter a scrap to anyone. We can let Abd-es-Salaam deal with it. Or Orhan Eser.'

'And Stevens?'

'Ah, well, that's a bit different. He's a British national.'

'Do you want me to carry on?'

'I'll ask the Old Man. You've written the report. That will keep London happy. All we need to do now is prod the Greeks occasionally. I mean, it's up to them now, isn't it? A crime on Greek territory? Not our pigeon.'

So that was it. After all the work he'd put in. Well, perhaps it wasn't *that* much work. All the same he felt sore. To bring him out here and then say, well, thank you very much. That's it, you can go now – even the equable Seymour was mildly irritated. And all over a cat. That was the worst thing about it. Think what they would say back at home! And how it would look on his record sheet. 'Invest-igated the death of a cat. Three weeks, Athens.' That would really help his career along, wouldn't it?

'You want to see Miriam?'

'Yes. The servant who fed the cat.'

Miriam was produced. Along with Talal, the eunuch, to interpret and keep things decent. This morning he was somewhat subdued. Perhaps he could sense that things were closing in.

'Miriam, I just want to –'

'Miriam, the Effendi just wanted to –'

'– take you back to the morning the cat died.'

'. . . cat died.'

'You put the bowl of milk down on the floor, if I remem-ber correctly?'

'That is so, Effendi.'

'And then Samira called you?'

'Yes, Effendi, she had lost her shoe, and I had been looking for it.'

'Did you find it?'

'In the end. It was in another room. How it got there, I do not know. Perhaps Chloe took it.'

'Chloe?'

'The little kitchen maid. We bring her into the harem sometimes, and Samira lets her play with her shoes. She likes to wear them and clop around and maybe –'

'It was only the one shoe that was lost, wasn't it?'

'Yes, it was one of a pair of golden shoes which Chloe liked especially and Samira always used to get them out for her.'

'Wouldn't she have been wearing both of them? If it had been Chloe?'

'Well, yes.'

'But it was just the one that was lost? Where was the other one?'

'Well, back in the Lady Samira's room, where it was supposed to be.'

'There's no special place for them, is there?'

'Yes, behind the curtain.'

'And that's where the other shoe was? Had you not looked there already?'

'Well, yes, Effendi, I had looked everywhere. And that was the place I looked first.'

'And when you did not find it, what did the Lady Samira do?'

'She was very angry. She said that she particularly wanted to wear those shoes that morning and told me to go on looking until I found them.'

'And you looked first in her room?'

'Yes, Effendi. Of course.'

'But didn't find it. But that had made you late, so then you had to run and get the milk?'

'Yes, Effendi.'

'And then when you came back, she called you and you had to start looking again?'

'That's right, Effendi.'

'In her room?'

'Well, yes, Effendi, because that's where they should be. But the Lady Samira called me a fool and said that I had already looked there, and she told me to look in some of the other rooms, and, of course, that's where I did find it, in the end, but, Effendi, I had looked before and am sure it had not been there –'

'Thank you, Miriam, that will be all.'

'It was not my fault, Effendi, and I have already been beaten over the milk, and it doesn't seem just that I should be beaten for the shoe as well –'

'Enough, woman, or you will be beaten again!' said Talal sternly, and hustled her out.

Seymour sat thinking, and then he sent for Leila.

'Leila, you do the Lady Irina's hair?'

'I do.'

'And you were doing it that morning when Miriam called to tell you that the cat was dying?'

'Dead, Effendi, just about dead!'

'Now, Leila, I am confused about the timing of all this. For you tell me that you were doing Irina's hair when Miriam called. And yet both Zenobia and the Lady Irina say that earlier, soon after the milk was brought, the Lady Irina had taken the cat into the adjoining room and was feeding it chocolates. Surely she could not have done that until *after* you had done her hair?'

'Not so, Effendi. She did it before, while she was waiting for me to do her hair.'

Talal could not contain himself.

'You mean – excuse me, Effendi – that the Lady Irina went into a public room *before* she had had her hair done?'

'That is so, yes.'

Talal turned to Seymour.

'Effendi, I cannot believe it! That would be indecent. To show her hair!'

'That's what she did,' said Leila doggedly.

'Effendi, I cannot accept this! This woman should be whipped –'

'She often does it,' said Leila. 'Especially if she has to wait. I try not to keep her waiting, she is so impatient. But that morning I had had to keep her waiting, because Samira was making such a fuss about her shoes. We were all looking for them, or rather, just the one shoe. How do you lose just one shoe? Anyway, she had us all looking for it, and I was late doing Irina's hair, and, as usual, she flew into a passion and stalked off into the room next to the salon, saying, "Someone's got to suffer for this! Where's that bloody cat?"'

'So the Lady Irina, and the cat, were not, at one point, in the room where the milk had been left?'

'She must have gone in to get the cat.'

'But then she took it next door?'

185

'Yes, Effendi. She likes to lie on the divan, with her hair all undone. Especially if she thinks the Sultan may be coming.'

'Leila,' burst in Talal, 'you can just cut out all this indecent talk!'

'It's true! She does, and he quite likes it.'

'Enough, Leila! Enough! This is going too far. Effendi, you will not believe what comes over these young women sometimes. You had better go, Leila. You have said enough. Has she not said enough, more than enough, Effendi?' Talal appealed to Seymour.

'I rather think she has,' said Seymour.

Next, Seymour summoned Chloe. She arrived quaking.

'It's all right, Chloe,' he reassured her. 'No one is angry with you. It is just that I have been thinking over what you told me and there is something I want to ask you.'

Chloe bobbed her head. She could barely speak.

'Chloe, I know you are a friend of the Lady Irina.'

'She spoke for me when the eunuchs would have beaten me.'

'So she did. I remember. And I remember that she took you on her lap and talked to you.'

'About my people.'

'Your people are the Vlachs, aren't they? Your uncle is a Vlach, and you are a Vlach. And I rather think the Lady Irina is a Vlach, too?'

'The Lady Irina is very beautiful.'

'I am sure she is. And she came from a village like you, didn't she?'

'The soldiers came.'

'Not to your village, fortunately, but certainly to hers. And to others, too. I know another lady who is also a Vlach and to whose village the soldiers came, long ago, and I would like you to meet her. Because I remember another thing you told me, Chloe, and that is that the Lady Irina said to you that the harem was no place for one such as yourself, and I think there may come a time, and it may come soon, when you will wish to seek for another place. This lady may help you.'

'I would have to do as my uncle bids me,' said Chloe.

'Of course. But I do not think he will object. Now, Chloe, as I said, there is something I wish to ask you. I know that the Lady Irina is your friend and I think that she may, occasionally, as a friend, ask you to do something for her.'

Chloe kept silent.

'It is a secret, of course. I appreciate that. But it is not a secret from me. Now, I think that the Lady Irina asked you to get a love potion for her. To gain her favour with the Sultan. And I think she told you that if you asked your uncle he would get it for you and that then you could take it secretly into the harem. And you were important, for only you could take it into the harem without the eunuchs knowing. As, I think, the Lady Irina told you.'

Chloe gazed at him, transfixed. Then she gave herself a little shake.

'Effendi,' she whispered, 'you know all. Or nearly all. But it was not quite as you said. The Lady Irina did indeed speak to me and I spoke to my uncle, as she commanded. And he obtained a love portion and brought it to me.

'But then, Effendi, it did not go as it was supposed to. For Amina heard us talking, my uncle and me, and after he had gone she took the potion from me.'

'*Amina* took it from you?'

'Yes, Effendi. She said she would give it to the Lady Samira, for the Lady Samira was more worthy to be the First Lady then Irina was, and she would give it to her.

'And I wept, Effendi, and tried to take it back, but she would not let me. And I went to the Lady Irina, weeping, for I knew I had let her down, and I did not want the Lady Samira to become First Lady of the harem. And I told the Lady Irina what had happened.'

'And what did the Lady Irina say?'

'She stood there, Effendi, for a long time, silent. And at

187

first I could see she was angry. And I told her she could beat me. But she didn't. She put her arms around me and said that it was nothing. But still I wept, for I knew I had failed her. And I told her this. But she went on holding me and seemed to be thinking, and then she said, "No, no, perhaps you have not failed. It may even be better like this." And she smiled. But, Effendi, it was not a smile such as she gives me.'

Seymour found Amina in her cubby-hole beneath the stairs. Although she was curled up and seemed to be sleeping, her eyes were open and looking at him maliciously.

'Amina,' he said, 'do you know what I think? I think you are the true mistress of the harem.'

She cackled with laughter.

'No, no,' she protested, 'I am but a servant. A kitchen maid, these days. The lowest of the low.'

'But Abd-es-Salaam values you. And I think he knows what he is doing.'

'Well, it may be as you say.'

'For it is your hand that plucks out the next senior wife.'

'No, no. Would it were so. I am nothing these days. Once, perhaps – but those days are long gone.'

'Nevertheless, you shape the future. For was it not you who took the potion meant for Irina and gave it to Samira?'

'The girl has told you?'

'Not all, perhaps.'

'No, not all. But I did take the potion from her. For why should Irina be the first? When Samira by right should be the one.'

'You gave the potion to Samira?'

'I did.' She cackled. 'To stiffen his rod. So that he will give Samira a baby. And she will rule in the harem.'

*   *   *

188

As Seymour was walking back up the corridor he saw Orhan Eser talking to Chloe just outside the kitchen door. He was bent over her and as Seymour watched, he saw him stroke her tenderly on the head. Then, hearing foot-steps, he hurried away quickly, and Chloe scuttled into the kitchen. When Seymour went in, she was away on the far side washing the dishes.

Seymour was now on confidential terms with the kitchen staff.

'Hello, Effendi!' they hailed him. 'Still on the trail?'

'On the trail of a good cup of tea,' he said.

'Well, Effendi, you have come to the right place. And, as it happens, the kettle has just boiled.'

Chloe hurried past him carrying a great pile of newly washed dishes. She disappeared through the door.

'It is good that Orhan Eser is kind to her,' Seymour said.

'Too kind,' one of the servants said tartly. 'What does he have in mind to do with her?'

'She is too young for that sort of thing,' said another servant disapprovingly.

'Ah, but his intentions are honourable,' said the senior servant. 'He has spoken to her uncle. I would not let Orhan Eser treat her thus otherwise.'

'Spoken to the uncle?' said another servant, amazed.

'So he told me.'

'Well, I would never have thought that! With one so young.'

'Perhaps he is planning ahead,' said someone.

'Or perhaps he just likes them young,' said another grimly.

'More biddable, certainly. But – surely she is not ready yet?'

'I would have thought not. But perhaps our eyes do not see.'

'It is not her doing,' said someone else, 'but her uncle's.'

'Well, it would be a good match for her.'

'But not for him. A man like Orhan Eser? So high and mighty? You would have thought he would have aimed higher.'

'And a Turk, too.'

'Orhan Eser likes Vlachs,' said Seymour. 'Or so I have heard.'

'Well, yes, but –'

'Orhan Eser is too grand for her,' said one of the servants. 'It will come to nothing.'

'What is he playing at?' asked someone.

'What is that foolish old man playing at!' said someone else indignantly. 'Sell off his niece . . .'

'His head has been turned!'

'Yes, but don't tell me that Orhan Eser's head has been turned! It's screwed on much too tight.'

'Well, be that as it may, they've come to an agreement. Orhan Eser and the old man.'

'Yes, but what agreement?'

Seymour finished his tea and left the kitchen. On his way out, he saw Talal, the eunuch, and on an impulse went up to him.

'Talal, a word in your ear. If I may.'

'Of course, Effendi.'

Seymour took him aside.

'Talal,' he said gravely, 'things are amiss around here.'

'They certainly are, Effendi. I reel.'

'I am not surprised, Talal. There are things which will have to be looked into. And who knows what may come out when they are?'

'Effendi, in all this I am guiltless!'

'Talal, I believe you. Yet there are those who would raise a questioning eye.'

'Let them look in other places.'

'Talal, you have hit upon it! There are other places which should be looked at.'

'The harem!' said Talal grimly.

'The kitchen!' said Seymour.

'Kitchen?'

'At any rate, other servants, too. Besides those in the harem.'

'Effendi, you speak truly. Very truly.'

'And the gaze should not stop with the low and humble. It should take in the mighty.'

'It should, Effendi. These are words of wisdom, indeed.'

'Talal, I would not ordinarily talk with you on such matters. For I know that you are loyal, discreet and true.'

'All these, Effendi, I am.'

'And it is not right for a man to come in and ask questions about others who are near to the one who is asked. Nevertheless, these are bad times.'

'Oh, they are, Effendi! They are.'

'Something must be done about the things that are amiss.'

'Effendi, you speak truly.'

'And I wondered if I could call on you?'

'Effendi, you can. Especially if it's a question of looking at others.'

'For you see all, Talal. In your position you see all.'

'Well, I do, Effendi.'

'The man I wish to ask about is Orhan Eser.'

'A man cleverer than he is just, Effendi.'

'Ah, you think so, too?'

'I know, Effendi. From bitter experience.'

'So I suspected. For people have told me that his favour falls on some and not on others.'

'And they have told you truly, Effendi.'

'On the Vlachs, for instance.'

'So people say.'

'But you have not observed it?'

'It is mostly outside the harem, Effendi. In the kitchen, I have heard, and with the cleaners.'

'But is not the Lady Irina a Vlach?'

'She is, Effendi.'

'I wondered if he had spoken with her?'

'He should not have done, Effendi. For he is outside the harem and she is in. And he is a male.'

'But things are amiss, Talal, and I wondered if he had?'

The eunuch was silent. Seymour guessed what he was thinking.

'I am not criticizing you, Talal. But sometimes it is hard to resist the command of one who is higher. Your words will go no further than my ears, Talal.'

'He *has* spoken with her. But . . .'

'Yes, Talal?'

'Not recently, Effendi. At one time he spoke with her a lot. It should not have been so, I know, Effendi, but, as you say, it is hard to resist the command of those who are higher than you are. And he has the ear of Abd-es-Salaam.'

'But he has not spoken to her so much recently?'

'No, Effendi. And – these words are for you alone – we have become concerned. For while he was talking to the Lady Irina we were comfortable, thinking that it meant that she was the one who was likely to catch the Sultan's favour and become first wife. But now he has stopped speaking to her. Now he speaks to Samira.'

Seymour, too, would like to speak to Samira; but first he would have to speak to Irina, and he wanted to speak to her not in anyone else's presence. That would be difficult, however possible it seemed to have been for Orhan Eser. And then he remembered something.

It was lunchtime and he caught Chloe as she came out of the kitchen carrying a great pile of dishes.

'Chloe! A word!'

'Effendi?'

'Chloe,' he said, 'you once told me that the Lady Irina had spoken to your uncle. How did she manage that?'

'There is a way –' began Chloe, but stopped.

'I would like to speak to her. In a way that no one would hear. It is important.'

'I would have to ask her.'

'Could you do that? Soon? As soon as you can?'

'I will try when I take the dishes. It depends on the eunuchs and whether they will let me in.'

'I will wait,' said Seymour.

Lunch had come and gone and everyone in the house was now at their siesta. The kitchen servants were either outside sprawled against the wall in the shade or had found some nook within the kitchen. Chloe came out of a door and took him by the hand.

'There is a grating in the wall,' she whispered. 'Come, I will show you.'

She took him into a small, disused scullery from which a door opened into the garden. The kitchen servants were round the corner and there was no one in sight. Chloe led him along the outside of the house to where a small grating had been set at knee level in the bricks.

'It is for air. The Lady Irina will be here tonight. At midnight. But she may be late because she will have to wait until everyone is asleep. Come into the courtyard and go to the right. I will be waiting.'

Seymour bent and looked at the grating. He tried it with his hand. It was firmly fixed.

'It is for air only,' whispered Chloe. 'But you can talk through it.'

Aphrodite joined him in the square for a cup of coffee on her way back from classes. It had almost become a custom now, one which he hoped was not confirming the expectation of others. This afternoon, though, she seemed cast down, depressed.

'Bad day?' he said sympathetically.

193

She shrugged.

'Something go wrong in the lab?'

She shrugged again.

'It's not that,' she said.

'What is it, then?'

'It's this business of Stevens. And Andreas's connection with it.'

'I wouldn't worry too much. It's awful when it happens, but he'll get over it.'

'No, no, it's – Popadopoulos came round again this morning, just before I left. Again! But this time he didn't want to talk to Andreas, he wanted to talk to my mother. And he just stayed there! I could see she didn't like it, so I stayed too. It made me late.'

'What was he talking to her about?'

'At first it was about Andreas. What a fine young man he was! How proud she must be, with him going to university! How were his studies going? Well, she shouldn't worry too much, a doctor's training was a long one and there was plenty of time for it all to come right.

'And then he asked her about the flying. What did she think of that? And, of course, she told him. Well, he said, mothers always feel like that. Young men always want to do exciting things, and mothers always have to watch them! But didn't she feel a thrill of pride at her son being one of the Blériot pilots? All of Athens felt pride. That we, the Greeks, a poor, ordinary country, should have flying machines? More flying machines than Britain or Germany? And brave, talented young men who flew them? Come on, he said, confess: doesn't it give you a thrill of pride to see your son up there?'

'"No," she said.

'That was because she wasn't seeing it with her son's eyes. To him it was all magical. And, indeed, it was magical. For the first time in history – if it was the first time and the story of Daedalus was just a myth – man had risen off the earth. Wasn't that magical? And wasn't it right that it should be the Greeks who were setting the pace? Because

194

Daedalus was *their* myth, flying, in a way, belonged to them.

'It *was* magical. He himself, Popadopoulos, felt it. When he had seen the machines close up! Had she been over there to see them? On the ground? Close up? Seen them as Andreas saw them? As something wonderful and exciting and strange and new?'

'And had she?' asked Seymour.

'Of course she had! Andreas pestered her until she agreed to go over there with him. They spent a morning there. He showed her everything, the Blériots, the one he flew. He even wanted her to get into the cockpit and see how it felt for herself. I think he would have taken her for a flight if she had agreed. She laughed, though, and said that sort of thing was all very well, but it was not for her.

'Popadopoulos laughed, too, when she told him, and said it wasn't for him, either! But it was right for Andreas to want to share it with her. It was important to him and good that he wanted her to share it. He, Popadopoulos, approved of that. That sort of thing kept families together, he said, and there wasn't enough of that these days.

'It was all so sympathetic and understanding. Kind, even. But –'

She broke off.

'But what?

'It made me uneasy. I felt he was up to something. I could see my mother felt that, too. And it made her uneasy.'

Chapter Thirteen

The wind had blown in the night and when Seymour went out everything was powdered with dust. The carriages were white as if with snow and the taste of grit hung in the air. Under foot the road was covered with a fresh layer of sand. It was like, he thought again, walking in the desert. The image shifted and became clearer. It was like walking in Istanbul. Athens and Istanbul, at times, were not far apart.

The sky this morning was clouded over with a dull haze from all the dust particles in the air: but, surprisingly, he heard the sound of flying machines. They were up early, flying over the city in close formation: one – two – three of them, all of them up there together at the same time in a show of bravado. They disappeared towards the mountains.

Seymour walked on towards the Sultan's residence, up the drive and past the three sets of guards. On either side of the drive the pines were powdered white, like Christmas trees half emerging through the snow.

In the courtyard, unusually, a dozen carriages were drawn up, their drivers chatting idly. Inside the house, however, the cavasses were hurtling around. They hardly had time to look at Seymour when he went in. He stood for a moment just inside the door and while he was waiting there Orhan Eser went past.

'What's up?' asked Seymour.

Orhan Eser pulled a face.

'The Sultan is sick again!' he said, and rolled his eyes.

He went on up the corridor. Seymour followed and saw a group of doctors waiting outside the Sultan's apartments. They, too, were chatting casually.

Seymour saw Dr Metaxas and went up to him.

'Again?' he said.

Dr Metaxas shrugged.

'Again!' he said.

The door opened and two frock-coated figures came out. Two other frock-coated figures went in. Apparently they were seeing the Sultan in turns.

'What's the point?' asked Seymour.

'None. But he likes to have second, third and fourth opinions and, since he's paying, we are happy to provide them.'

'Anything different?' someone asked one of the doctors who had just come out.

The doctor shrugged.

'Not as far as I can see,' he said.

They all seemed relieved, amused, even. No one seemed to be taking the Sultan's plight very seriously.

'Stomach pains again?'

'So he says. Poisoned, of course!'

They all laughed.

'I'm fed up with this nonsense,' said Dr Metaxas. 'This time I'm going to say it's just wind.'

'Why don't you tell him it's gastro-enteritis?' asked one of the doctors. 'It sounds more impressive. And serious. Then we can go on coming.'

'I don't *want* to go on coming,' said Dr Metaxas. 'It's a ridiculous waste of time!'

'Tell him it's just wind and that will certainly be an end of *your* coming,' said someone.

'None of us will be coming,' said someone else, 'soon.'

'Why is that?' asked Seymour.

They looked at each other.

'It's just that – well, no one's interested any longer. It doesn't matter any more, now that the war has actually started.'

'The war has started?'

'Yes. The soldiers marched off this morning.'

'But they've marched off before!'

'It's serious this time.'

'Don't they need an excuse? I mean, wasn't that the point of everyone being worried about the Sultan?'

'They've decided they don't need one. Or perhaps they've found another one. Whatever it is, no one's interested in the Sultan any more.'

'So they won't be interested in *us*,' said one of the doctors.

'Will he go on paying, do you think?' asked someone.

'Wouldn't have thought so.'

'Then I won't be interested in *him*!' declared another doctor, to general nods.

Abd-es-Salaam, grim-faced, came through the door.

'How is he?' asked Seymour.

'That's not the point,' said the Acting-Vizier. 'The point is, they are removing the guards!'

'Are the guards necessary?' asked Orhan Eser, who was standing waiting for him.

'Ours are!' said Abd-es-Salaam. 'Doubly necessary now that they're removing the others. This is the moment for someone to strike.'

Orhan Eser shrugged dismissively.

A little later Seymour saw him standing with the Acting-Vizier outside the open front door of the house, looking up into the sky.

'They're flying again,' he said.

'Does that mean that the fighting has started?' asked Seymour.

'Possibly.'

'How will that affect you?' asked Seymour.

Orhan Eser looked at Abd-es-Salaam.

'That depends,' he said.

'I shall have to clarify the Sultan's position,' said the Acting-Vizier. 'In the new circumstances.'

He turned and went back inside the house.

'What about you?' Seymour said to Orhan Eser. 'Will you go back to Istanbul?'

'I hope so,' said Orhan Eser. 'I am a soldier, not . . .' He hesitated. 'Whatever this is,' he said, and went after Abd-es-Salaam.

Seymour went out into the courtyard and chatted to the guards. After a while the doctors started coming out and getting into their carriages. Dr Metaxas was the last. He came out some time after the others, so much so that Seymour thought he had missed him. At last, though, he came down the steps.

'I have been talking to Orhan Eser,' he said. '"Maybe it's our last chance," I said, "because I won't be coming again." "And if you did," he said, "you probably wouldn't find me. Because I'm going back to Istanbul." "Job done?" I said. He shrugged. "Who knows?" he said. "At any rate, my part of it is done. Goodness knows what they'll do with the old Sultan now. He'll have to leave Greece, that's clear. But he can hardly go back to Salonica just now, with the Greeks marching on it."

'"And what about you?" I said. "What are you going to do now?" "Oh, I'll go back to being a soldier," he said. "I hope they'll give me something to do with transport again. It's simpler, mucking about with carts and cars. I've been away from that sort of thing too long." And then he said something that surprised me. He said, "I'm glad we've met. Just now when the war is starting, because it reminds me of that time when we worked together up in the mountains. And that's a good thing to remember when you're just going to fight somebody. That it's possible to work together. Because that means that maybe one day you will."

'I thought that was good, you know? It made me glad that I'd talked to him. We shook hands. "Take care of yourself," he said, "and don't let them drag you back in. I can't help it because I'm a soldier. But you don't have to be."'

They walked back up the drive together and when they got to the end Dr Metaxas suggested they walk a bit further and have a drink in Constitution Square.

'It will give you a chance to meet Aphrodite,' he said slyly. 'She's coming home early and it is too much to be hoped for that her mother will not send her to fetch me.'

Seymour had been thinking about Aphrodite ever since his conversation with Farquhar. The end of the case meant the end of his being out here and the end of his . . . whatever it was, with Aphrodite. And that meant he had to face it. Or – and this was more likely, he realized with a flash of self-insight, find out a way of *not* facing it.

Of course, that meant facing up to the family, too.

'You know,' he said, 'things are coming to an end for me, too, out here.'

Dr Metaxas nodded. 'The Sultan?'

'They've lost interest. And I know what happened, anyway.'

'The cat?'

'I know who killed it.'

Dr Metaxas nodded again.

'Then things are at an end for you,' he said, 'out here.'

The wind was still stirring the dust and there were not many people sitting at the tables in the square. Mostly they were inside the large cafés around its edges. A few carriages were moving but most were stationary, the horses standing with their heads down, the drivers huddled inside their cabs. The only people about were the small bootblacks who rushed on them indomitably to feather the dust from their boots.

'English?' one of them said to Seymour.

'That's right.'

The boy looked up at the sky.

'No sun,' he said. 'Like England.'

'Like England,' Seymour agreed, reaching into his pocket for a few drachmas.

'The soldiers have gone?' he asked.

'Gone this morning. Halfway to Salonica by now.'

'Halfway back, too,' said another of the boys cynically.

Dr Metaxas led the way to one of the cafés and they went inside. The warmth and the noise and the tobacco smoke hit Seymour like a blow. He would have preferred, despite the cold, to sit outside but Dr Metaxas shrugged it all off and found a table. They obviously knew him for they at once put an ouzo before him. Since Seymour was with him, they put one for Seymour, too, and, this morning Seymour was glad of it. Fortunately they brought coffee, too.

Everyone was talking about the war.

'It's started, then.'

'The sooner it gets started, the sooner it'll get finished,' seemed to be the general attitude.

Dr Metaxas listened sceptically.

The door opened and Aphrodite came in.

'Found you!' she pounced.

'All right,' said Dr Metaxas resignedly. 'I'll come quietly. But not for a minute,' he added.

'Very well,' said Aphrodite, sitting down. 'You can finish your drink.'

'Can I finish mine, Aphrodite?' asked someone at the next table, who evidently knew them.

'No!' said Aphrodite, laughing. 'Give it to me!'

The man slipped it across to her good-naturedly and called for another one. He raised it:

'To victory!' he said.

'Or defeat!' said Dr Metaxas, raising his glass, too.

'Why defeat?' asked someone at the next table.

'Because that will see the end of Venizelos and his daft ideas,' said Dr Metaxas.

'Say what you like about Venizelos,' said someone, 'but –'

And the arguments, as usual roared away.

'I think I've found someone,' Aphrodite said to Seymour.

'Found –?' said Dr Metaxas.

'A home for a little girl.'

'Finding homes for people?' asked Dr Metaxas, amazed. 'Are you into that, now?'

'I'm sorry,' said Seymour. 'Blame me. I asked Aphrodite if she knew anyone –'

'It's a little girl,' said Aphrodite, 'and she works in the Sultan's kitchen.'

'She's a Vlach,' said Seymour, 'and I thought –'

'It's not right for a young girl to be so close to a harem!' said Aphrodite. 'Who knows what pressure may be put on her?'

'Actually,' said Seymour, 'there's been a development.'

He told them about Orhan Eser.

'Orhan Eser?' said Dr Metaxas, surprised. 'But he's already married! He told me so himself. Just this morning.'

'He's a Muslim,' said Seymour.

'But that – that makes it worse!' cried Aphrodite. 'A second wife! And at that age! We've got to do something,' she said to her father.

'Got to?' said Dr Metaxas.

'Got to,' said Aphrodite firmly. 'Can we sit by and let this sort of thing happen in Athens?'

'It happens all the time in Athens,' said Dr Metaxas.

'Well, I'm against it,' said Aphrodite. 'I'm against arranged marriages and all that goes with it. Marrying off young girls, girls barely more than children, before they've

202

– It's backward. It harks back to Ottoman days. It's a practice we should get rid of! And here's a chance for us to do something.'

'She's a Vlach,' said Seymour, 'and so is her uncle. That's why I thought –'

'He should be ashamed of himself!' said Aphrodite indignantly.

'Of course, it's none of my business really –' said Seymour.

'What would Mother say?' demanded Aphrodite.

'Well –'

'I know what she would say. She would say: Vlach or Ottoman, we cannot allow this sort of thing to happen!'

'She probably would,' agreed Dr Metaxas. He looked at Seymour. 'You may not have noticed, but there's a considerable resemblance between my wife and her daughter. Both are impetuous and inclined to rush wildly in when their feelings are engaged. Over the years I have had some success in getting my wife to moderate her feelings; but with Aphrodite . . .!' He shook his head.

'Father, you know you don't agree with these practices. They belong to the past and the sooner they're in the past, the better!'

'Yes, yes.'

'You surely don't think we should do nothing!'

Dr Metaxas held up a hand. 'What I think doesn't matter, since you say you've found somebody.'

'Eva, I thought.'

'I'm not sure about that. Perhaps you should speak to your mother.' He stopped. 'On second thoughts, perhaps you should not. Not just at the moment!' He looked at Seymour. 'She is not herself. This business of Andreas. And the war. It takes her back – back to bad days.'

'Please forget all about it,' said Seymour. 'I shouldn't have mentioned it. Not to you, at this time, at any rate.'

'No, no –'

'It's just that, as she is a Vlach –'

'Quite right. We should do something about it. She would want us to. It's just that –'

'Forget I spoke.'

'She is not herself. These things, coming together and now the little girl. The harem. I fear it would take her back. You think those things are past,' he said bitterly, 'but they're never past. Suddenly something happens and they come back on you.'

He got up and went out, leaving his drink upon the table.

'A bit late to be visiting, isn't it, sir?' said the petty officer at the gates. It was the only challenge he had received in his progression up the drive. The other guards appeared to have been withdrawn.

'Someone is expecting me,' said Seymour.

There had been a lot of to-ing and fro-ing that day, what with the Sultan's illness, and the petty officer thought that this was more of the same. Besides, he had got used to Seymour now and Seymour was, after all, an Englishman, which, among so many dubious foreigners, was in itself a guarantee of respectability. He waved him on through.

The courtyard was dark, and there appeared to be no lights on in the house. He went up to it and bore right as Chloe had directed him. And almost at once she was there, putting her hand on his arm and guiding him round the outside of the house. It was pitch-dark and without her aid he wouldn't have managed. Even when they reached the grille she had to guide his hand so that he would feel it.

He put his ear to the grille and then, when he could hear nothing, he whistled softly into it. But there was no response.

'She is not there yet,' Chloe whispered into his ear.

They sat down beside the grille and waited. They sat like that for close on an hour, and then he was suddenly conscious of Chloe leaning forward and listening intently. She blew into the grille and then pulled his face down and pressed her cheek against the ironwork. He felt the breathing the other side rather than heard it.

'Irina?'

'So,' she said, 'we are cheek to cheek! Almost. Samira would be envious.'

'Never mind Samira. It's you I want to talk to.'

'But you only want to talk to me about unimportant things. Like cats.'

'And Sultans.'

'When I was first taken to the harem,' said Irina, 'I was twelve. And at that time I thought Sultans were important.'

'And now you think differently?'

'It was very interesting when the revolution came and the Sultan was deposed. Suddenly I realized that a lot of people felt differently. It came as a surprise to me.'

'And now he is unimportant.'

'I had found that out long before. And yet, in a way, he is important. To me. Without him I would be free. When they exiled him, they set free most of the harem. They advertised – yes, actually advertised – come and get your daughter! And, of course, a lot of people came, although by this time they often did not recognize their daughter. But they let the Sultan choose the ones he wanted to keep and I was one of the ones. I had no say in the matter. It was all decided for me. And when he was sent to Salonica, we were sent with him.

'I thought perhaps I would be able to speak to someone and say I did not want to go, but it did not work out like that. One day we were taken out of the harem and put in closed carriages and we stayed shut in until we reached the new house in Salonica. And suddenly I realized that it was going to go on.

'I had thought that maybe the English or the French or the Greeks – my people had always been close to the Greeks, after all – would intervene and say, "No, you can't do that! You must let her go." But, of course, we were too small. We didn't count in the scheme of things. The new

Government in Istanbul had other things on its mind and the British and the French were so relieved that the things were being sorted out without a war that they weren't going to make a fuss over a few details. Like us.

'And then when we moved from Salonica to Athens, I thought: the Greeks, we are going to Greece, the Greeks will do it! They know what the Ottomans are like, and they hate the Sultan as much as I do.

'But they didn't. They, too, had other things on their mind, and for them the Sultan was important and not us. They put walls around him and guards. But they were also putting walls around us. I wanted to speak to someone but couldn't. I couldn't even get close enough to arrange to be able to tell them. I suddenly realized I was trapped, still trapped; and in my heart I felt that it would be forever.'

'And so,' said Seymour, 'you decided that the only way out was to kill the Sultan?'

She was silent for so long that he thought she must have moved away or that someone had found her.

But at last she spoke.

'I have grown wary. I have learned my lesson,' she said. 'If I do something for you, you must do something for me.'

'Of course I will do anything I can.'

'Oh, no,' she said. 'That's not good enough. You want me to tell you what has been happening here. And I will tell you. But first – first! – you must do what I want.'

'What do you want?'

'I want to be free.'

'I will do everything I can.'

'Will you set me free?'

'I don't really have the power.'

'Of course you don't. You are, in the end, just a little person, like me. But you must talk to the people who sent you from London. For them to send you here, there must be something here that is important to them. Perhaps it is even the Sultan. It is hard to think why he should be important to them, or to anyone. But if you want my help

206

you must go to them and say: set her free. When she is free, she will tell you everything you want to know. But first you must set her free.'

And then she was gone.

Seymour sat back on his heels. It was not what he had expected. He had thought that, knowing so much, he would have her in a corner. But somehow she had wriggled out of it, had turned the tables. And he couldn't but admire her. With apparently no card to play, she had somehow plucked one out of the air.

But it wouldn't work. The card was in the end too small. Things had changed. They didn't care any more: about him or her. She was just too small.

He felt deeply sorry for her. He would do what he could. He suspected, though, that it would not be enough. In the end she was just too small. The Great Powers were too great to be interested. He would try, but he knew he wouldn't get anywhere.

Unless – an idea suddenly came to him.

Popadopoulos leaped up and embraced him warmly.

'The man himself! Not ten days in the city and already at the heart of all the intrigue!'

'Off on the flanks, I would say,' said Seymour, sitting down. 'And –' thinking of the night before – 'in a backwater, becalmed.'

'Backwater? Ah, no, my friend: I insist. At the centre. As it turns out.'

'As it turns out?'

The dust of the previous day had blown itself out and away and the morning was fresh and bright. The oranges in the little garden almost sparkled in the early sun and pleasant aromas of coffee drifted over the tables. The tables were already full of people getting on with – well, actually, not getting on with anything much. Life, that is, was back to normal.

When he had got back to the hotel last night he had

found a note awaiting him which suggested that he and Popadopoulos should meet for breakfast; which he was rather glad that they should do.

Popadopoulos this morning was full of energy, indeed, high spirits.

'Getting somewhere,' he said, with satisfaction. 'I think.'

He told Seymour that he had been pursuing the matter of the cut cables.

'As I told you, I thought that would be easier. For how many people in Athens know enough about the Blériot flying machines to be able to cut their cables? Know enough to know that that would be the thing to do if you wanted to disable them? Not me, certainly. All the aeronautical mechanics in Athens can be counted on the fingers of two hands. A car mechanic? Yes, possibly, and there are rather more of them. But not that many more. So, I said, let us begin with the cables.'

'And you have got somewhere?'

'I think so. Although where I have got will, I think, surprise you.'

'Okay, surprise me.'

'First, though, the nature of that first attack. Was it directed against George's machine or against the Blériots in general? It was certainly not directed personally against Stevens, for he could have been flying in any of the Blériots, and would he have been flying, anyway? If he had been the target, the attack would have been more . . . specific.

'So, the Blériots in general. That makes it look more of a military matter, an attempt at sabotage. As, of course, everyone on the base assumed. An Ottoman spy or agent, perhaps.

'That, at least, gave me something to look for, narrowed the search down. Not just someone with the technical know-how to be able to target the cables, but also, probably, an Ottoman or Ottoman sympathizer. Alas, though, there are not many Ottoman sympathizers in Athens, and those that are are not very interested in flying machines. It seems a Greek phenomenon. Of course, there will be some and there could be a mechanic among them, and I thought that they would be sufficiently uncommon for people in that line of work to know of them. That was not apparently so, however; and perhaps that in itself is significant. It might mean that the person I was looking for was not a regular mechanic. Regular,' he repeated with emphasis, looking at Seymour. Meaningfully, Seymour thought.

'My thoughts then turned to the second attack. And this was different. For it was quite clearly aimed at a particular individual. It depended on knowledge of Stevens' tastes and habits – very particular knowledge, extending to his taste in milk. But who would possess such detailed personal knowledge? Bearing in mind how few people Stevens knew in Athens. It could only be one of those who worked with him; or at the very least someone who was very close to one of them.'

'Maria,' said Seymour. 'I thought at first that it might be Maria. My mind has been running on similar lines to yours. She knew about the arrangements for the milk – she had set them up. And she would have had opportunity. But –'

Popadopoulos nodded.

'Yes,' he said, 'I thought of Maria, too. At first.'

'I even wondered if she was a Vlach,' said Seymour, 'and in on that network of connections. I asked her husband. But she isn't.'

'Yes,' said Popadopoulos, 'there seems to be a Vlach connection, doesn't there? The arrangements for delivering the milk, the knowledge that lies behind it. That was my thought, too. And let us continue with the thought and see where it carries us.

'The only Vlach among Stevens' colleagues, indeed, the only Vlach on the base, is Andreas Metaxas. He certainly knew about Stevens' taste in milk. And he would certainly have had the opportunity to put poison in the milk. He was there all night, on his own, sleeping beside the flying machines. He and Stevens might have had breakfast together. He could even have volunteered to make up the flask for Stevens.

'There is one other thing. Why have we not been able to find the flask? It would have been helpful to have found it because that would have confirmed the poison and the means. But the flask has disappeared. Might not Andreas have thrown it over the side of the cockpit?

'Speculation, speculation: but what is not speculation is that the milk was poisoned and the poison was probably put in during the night and that Andreas was the only person there during the night.'

'But –' began Seymour.

'Exactly!' said Popadopoulos. 'But.'

'Andreas idolized Stevens,' said Seymour. 'He even took him home to persuade his family.'

'True. There is also the question of motive. And it is hard to think of anyone with less motive for killing Stevens than Andreas.'

Popadopoulos drank up his coffee and then signalled to the waiter for more.

'So let us turn our thoughts in a different direction. Andreas is not the only Vlach to take into consideration. We have to take into account his family, and in particular his mother.'

'But, surely –'

Popadopoulos held up a finger.

'One moment: unlikely, yes, but not impossible. A Vlach herself, part of that intimate network, she might well know the arrangement for delivering the milk; and if she didn't of her own accord, Andreas might well have told her. She has not been sleeping well lately, indeed, has been going for long nocturnal walks. Might she not have walked as far as the base? And, knowing, as she did, the movements of the milkman, timed her arrival for after the milk had been delivered and while it was still waiting outside with the stone over the top?

'We have to say: knowledge of very particular details,

210

confined only to a few, opportunity to administer the poison and – it has to be said, unlike her son – strong motive. She feared for her son. Hated his flying. Hated war. Did not like Stevens and blamed him not just for her son's flying but for the probability of his going to war. Yes, Andreas was flying, anyway; but would he have seen himself as flying in the war? Stevens was encouraging it, without him it might not have happened. Without him it might not continue happening.

'And remember, these are not the ordinary misgivings of an ordinary mother. They are the misgivings of someone who knows only too well what war is. Of someone who cares passionately, possibly over-passionately, for her son. And of course who is, how shall I put it, just at the moment in a very disturbed frame of mind.'

'Look,' said Seymour, 'I can see what you're saying, and can go along with it up to a point, although I'm not sure that I would go as far as saying that Mrs Metaxas was so disturbed as to contemplate killing someone. But aren't you forgetting one thing? The cable-cutting. That rather goes along with it. Are you seriously suggesting that Mrs Metaxas has the technical knowledge and expertise to –'

'No,' said Popadopoulos, 'I am not. But I am suggesting that she might have had the help of someone who unquestionably does have the knowledge and expertise, and who has, indeed, worked specifically on Blériots: her daughter.'

Seymour went silent.

Popadopoulos stood up.

'And so, you see, you *are* at the heart of things. You have become close to the Metaxas family. Close – how close? – to Aphrodite.' He put his hand on Seymour's shoulder. 'Think over all that has happened since you arrived in Athens. Consider it in the light of what I have just said.'

He patted Seymour gently on the shoulder and then walked away.

Chapter Fourteen

'Of course, I have every sympathy,' said the Ambassador.

But, supplied Seymour silently.

'But,' said the Ambassador, 'I don't see how we can intervene. We don't have a *locus*. She is not a British national, she is not on British territory, she does not, as far as I can see, come under any international agreement to which we are party.'

'But, surely, sir,' said Seymour, 'her status is bound up with that of the Sultan –'

'Well, that is confusing enough.'

'But the Great Powers, and among them Britain, *have* taken on responsibility for the Sultan –'

'– de facto,' said Farquhar helpfully.

'– to an extent,' said the First Secretary. 'Only to an extent.'

'It's the extent that's the problem,' said the Ambassador, 'and whether it reaches to the harem of an ex-Sultan –'

'Doubtful, sir,' said the First Secretary.

'I could take guidance, I suppose,' said the Ambassador thoughtfully. 'From London. Although it's all so complicated that I'm not sure they would wish to bother.'

'Leave it to your discretion, sir,' said Farquhar.

'Thank you very much, Farquhar. Let's not put *that* idea into their head.'

'Of course, once the matter of the Sultan himself is resolved, it should be easy,' said the First Secretary. 'But that could take some time.'

'I don't think we can just leave her in limbo, sir,' objected Seymour.

'Why not?' said the First Secretary. 'It's where the ex-Sultan is.'

'And a very useful place for him to be,' said the Ambassador. 'Limbo. That is to say he is in a place where we haven't yet made up our mind exactly where it is but probably will one day. And that's a fair description of the situation, isn't it? And at least it's something. Better than nothing. Just. The point is, it's a working solution, something that everyone can go along with.'

'But she'd still be there, sir,' protested Seymour.

'Well, there is that.'

'Seymour, I don't see why you're making such an issue of this,' said the First Secretary. 'You say you know who poisoned the cat. And you seem to have a pretty good idea of who was responsible for the attacks on the Sultan. Why is a deal with this person necessary?'

'It's a question of proof.'

'Do we need to be too fussy about that? Why not simply make public what you know?'

'Because if I do, the person may be killed.'

'Hmm,' said the Ambassador.

'Seymour, is that any concern of yours? Taking the large view?'

'Well, we wouldn't like to see –' began the Ambassador.

'Surely that can be left to the law,' said the First Secretary.

'Yes,' said Seymour, 'but *what* law? You, yourself, sir, have said that she is in limbo. What kind of law applies in limbo? Especially this one? Greek? Ottoman? International?'

'Well, that is a tricky point, I agree.'

'And while it is being settled, if I go public, she might be killed under the Sultan's law!'

'Hmm,' said the Ambassador.

There was a prolonged silence.

The First Secretary was shaking his head.

'Any deal, sir, would have to be an international one. All the Powers would have to agree.'

'No chance,' said the Ambassador. 'Whatever the subject.'

'Perhaps limbo, sir,' suggested the First Secretary, 'is a good place for it to be left in?'

'Of course, I have every sympathy . . .' said the Ambassador.

But.

'Yes,' said Samira, 'I killed the cat.'

'Lady Samira!' cried Talal. 'Think what you are saying!'

'Shut up, Talal! I know what I am saying. And Mr Seymour knows what I am saying, too. Don't you, Mr Seymour?'

'Yes,' said Seymour.

'The game is up, Talal. But it gave spice to life for a time. Which you certainly don't, Talal. But now the game is up.'

'I don't think it need be, Lady Samira,' said Seymour.

'No?' she said, surprised.

'Different people want different things,' he said. 'So perhaps all could be satisfied. The Lady Irina, for instance, wants to get out of the harem. Whereas I don't think you quite want that, do you?'

'Sometimes I do. But, of course, if the Lady Irina left –'

'You could be the chief wife, couldn't you? In fact, you have been working to that end.'

'It is true that my thoughts have occasionally tended in that direction.'

'You thought that if you killed the cat and got Irina blamed for it, then that would finish her as a rival.'

'It certainly wouldn't help her. Particularly if I hinted – just hinted, you know – that she was only practising.'

'And she definitely did have the Sultan in mind,' said Seymour.

'Oh, yes. There was no secret about it. She was furious

214

when she heard he was taking her to Salonica. "Why don't you let me go?" she said. But he wouldn't let her go. For some reason, which I have never understood, he wanted to keep her. She must have been doing some perverse thing with him which I have not been able to find out. For her natural charms are few.'

'Lady Samira, I do not think you should speak of the Sultan in this way –'

'Shut up, Talal. Just because your natural charms have been taken away –'

'Lady Samira,' said Seymour, 'you knew that Irina planned to secure her freedom by poisoning the Sultan. And you knew, somehow, that Chloe was bringing the poison in for her.'

'I overheard Irina talking to Chloe's uncle at that grating. If only I had known about that grating earlier! Talal, why didn't you tell me about the grating?'

'I didn't know about the grating,' said Talal sulkily.

'But that little Chloe did. The slyboots! Anyway, I overheard Irina and the milkman – those Vlachs! How they stick together! And I kept my eye on little Chloe, and when she tried to bring the stuff in I took it from Amina.'

'And then you used it.'

'Exactly.'

'Miriam brought the milk into the harem –'

'And then I called her to look for my shoes. Which I had carefully hidden. And then I suddenly remembered where they might be and sent her to look for them.'

'Which gave you a chance to slip out and put poison in the bowl –'

'– while Irina was feeding the cat with chocolates in an attempt to make it sick over the Sultan.'

'The cat died –'

'– and I took care to hint that the Sultan could be the real target. That worked amazingly well. The poor man even developed stomach pains! Unfortunately, that meant that the next minute the house was full of doctors and police-men, so I decided to lie low. They even brought in a policeman from England!

'And then I had a brainwave. I would get *him* to suggest that Irina had done it. I would plant the idea in his mind. That would be fun. Much more fun that planting ideas in your mind, Talal, where to plant any idea would be an uphill task.

'So I did. I planted ideas in Mr Seymour's mind. Unfor-tunately he did more with them than I had intended. Let that be a lesson to you, Talal. You cannot rely upon a policeman when it comes to ideas. Especially an English policeman.'

She held out her wrists.

'Well, bind me and take me to Abd-es-Salaam. What will it be, do you think, Talal? The garotte?'

'Not so fast, Lady Samira!' said Seymour. 'That may not be necessary. It rather depends on you.'

'On me, Mr Seymour?'

'On you, and what you can tell me.'

'She will tell you anything you want, Effendi,' said Talal.

'Ah, but it has to be the truth.'

'She will find that more difficult, Effendi.'

Samira smiled sweetly. Seymour could see that because during the conversation the veil had slipped entirely from her face.

'What is it you wish to know, Mr Seymour?'

'Orhan Eser spoke to you: I want to know what he spoke about.'

Samira deliberated. Then she looked Seymour straight in the face. (This, too, was unseemly and Talal was about to remonstrate: but then he thought better.)

'He asked me to give him some of the poison that I had taken from Chloe.'

'And did you?'

216

'I did.'

'Thank you. It may be necessary for you to swear to that. But if you do, I shall speak to Abd-es-Salaam in your favour and I think he may be willing then to show you mercy.'

'Orhan Eser,' said Seymour, 'I have some questions I wish to put to you.'

'Questions?' said the Acting-Vizier's assistant, startled. 'Me?'

'The first is why you asked the Lady Samira for some of the poison she had taken from the servant girl, Chloe?'

Orhan Eser thought for a moment.

'I took it lest it be used to harm His Royal Highness.'

'Then why did you not take all of it?'

'I did take all of it.'

'The Lady Samira will swear otherwise.'

'The Lady Samira is not to be trusted.' Orhan Eser paused. 'In any case,' he said, 'the oath of a woman counts less than the oath of a man under our laws and I shall swear against her.'

'Ah, but I, too, will swear; about what she told me. And I am a man. And there is another witness, too. Also a man. Two men against one, Orhan Eser.'

He waited. Orhan Eser said nothing.

'There is another thing, too. You left Samira with some of the poison. Why was that, if it was not that you were content for her to use it?'

'She was going to use it against the cat.'

'Only? That is the question I will ask, Orhan Eser; and it may be that Abd-es-Salaam will ask it, too.'

'Then I shall answer it.'

'Before you spoke with the Lady Samira, you spoke, several times, with the Lady Irina. What was that about?'

'I do not recall.'

'Did she speak to you about wanting to leave the harem?

217

Mind how you answer; for it may be that Irina will swear to this, too.'

'She did speak about that, yes.'

'And did she also say that if she were not allowed to leave the harem, she might harm the Sultan?'

'I do not think so.'

'I am asking this because I am wondering how you knew that Chloe was bringing poison into the harem. Did the Lady Irina tell you that she had asked for it? Tell you in her desperation?'

'No.'

'Whether she did or not does not perhaps much matter. For somehow you learned about it. And did not report it. Why was that, Orhan Eser? That is the question I shall ask; and, I think, Abd-es-Salaam, too. There is much that you have not reported, Orhan Eser.'

'One cannot report everything,' Orhan Eser muttered.

'And here is another question, Orhan Eser. It concerns the agreement you came to with the old man about his niece, Chloe. You agreed that you would marry her; in return for what, Orhan Eser? In return for what?'

'For the girl.'

'I think not, Orhan Eser. And this we can ask the old man. And I think he will tell us. He is a Vlach, Orhan Eser, and what does he care for your Ottoman machinations?'

Orhan Eser was silent.

'It would have been a handsome marriage for a servant girl, would it not? A man like yourself! You were giving much. What was he giving?'

Orhan Eser did not reply.

'Shall I tell you what I think you got? You got help. With the poisoning of the Englishman who looked after the flying machines – those flying machines which had troubled you when you had seen them overhead – troubled you so much that, although this was hardly your job, you had complained to the British Embassy about them.'

'Nonsense!' said Orhan Eser, running the tip of his tongue over his lips. 'I did not complain –'

'Ah, but the Embassy will say you did. And their word, when weighed against yours? Along with so much else?'

Seymour waited.

'Shall I tell you, Orhan Eser, what I think the deal was? You asked for help in poisoning Stevens Effendi. Perhaps you asked for poison, either before you got it from Chloe – maybe that was not enough – or after. You may even have asked him to put the poison in the milk – the milk that only Stevens drank, and which you knew about.'

'Why should I do this?' asked Orhan Eser.

'Because you are a soldier,' said Seymour. 'As you once told me and as you told others. You have always been a soldier and you think as a soldier.

'It was as a soldier that you looked at the flying machines. You saw how they could be used in a war and how they might be used by the Greeks. And you decided to do something about it. You had a background in military transport and technical know-how. Although you had no first-hand experience of Blériots, it would be easy for you to understand how they could be disabled. And one night you went to the base and cut the cables. And later, when that was not enough, as a soldier you killed Stevens.'

'I was a soldier once, but –' said Orhan Eser.

'And are a soldier still,' said Seymour. 'And your loyalty is not to the Sultan but to those who think like you and now rule in Istanbul.'

Orhan Eser did not, in the end, seek to deny it. He was, as he was proud to admit, still a soldier and when he had seen the need and the opportunity to strike a blow for his country, he had struck. He had not deceived Dr Metaxas. His views were, indeed, on the modern, reforming side – except when it came to women, he had never really

219

intended to marry Chloe – but when the old, eternal hostility between Greek and Turk had reopened, the old loyalty had reasserted itself.

Everything he had done, he insisted, had been on his own initiative. His Government back in Istanbul had had nothing to do with it, something that they at once indignantly corroborated. But, then, they would, wouldn't they?

It was a neat point whether Orhan Eser had diplomatic immunity. Did the Sultan's house count as a diplomatic posting? Seymour had no intention of involving himself in any debate of that sort and happily handed it over to the diplomats. But he did have quite a long discussion with Abd-es-Salaam.

With so many problems on his agenda the Acting-Vizier was only too glad to dispose of some of them and on Seymour's advice the Lady Irina was allowed to leave the harem. For a while she was strangely at a loss for such a formidable lady but then Aphrodite took her under her wing and the last time she was heard of she was doing very well as a student at university.

Again on Seymour's advice, the Lady Samira's sins were forgiven her. The Acting-Vizier had never much cared for the cat, either. Besides, with Irina gone the issue of who was top cat in the harem could be swiftly resolved and what was left of the harem now entered upon a period of stability, although not, alas, harmony, under Samira.

Chloe left the Sultan's employment and took up a position first with the Metaxas family and then with another Vlach household; which Irina visited from time to time. After a crisp exchange between her and Chloe's uncle, the old man abandoned forever any idea of arranging a marriage for his niece. On Popadopoulos's advice, he henceforth confined his carrying, whether of milk or poison, to the mountains.

Popadopoulos enjoyed a brief period of popularity in

Athens as the man who got the man who had tried to interfere with their beloved flying machines, but then fell foul of Greek politics.

The war did actually start and the Greek soldiers did actually seize Salonica. In fact, they seized a great deal more and the collapsing Ottoman Empire was forced into major territorial concessions; concessions which they mostly took back a few years later when the Greeks pushed their luck a step too far and landed an army in Anatolia, whereupon they were soundly defeated and the Balkans returned for a while to peace and tranquillity. For about five minutes, actually.

For a while, too, things looked very promising between Seymour and Aphrodite; but then life intervened. Aphrodite had to stay in Athens to support her mother while Andreas was away at the war, and Seymour had to return to England. He promised to come back when he had his next holiday, but he never had a holiday. A couple of big jobs came up, first in one part of the world and then in another, and just when he thought he had finally made it, it was 1914 and he had other things on his mind.

It was then that, sitting in the trenches, and watching the flying machines overhead, he began to think that possibly Stevens had been right after all about the use that might be made of them in a war, and that things might have been different. But by then, of course, it was too late.